"So are you still spouse-hunting in Riviera waters, Olivia?" Luc asked.

"I would be if you hadn't robbed us of our trip!" she replied. "It's only fair you make up for it now. Who knows? I might meet an exciting playboy with husband potential! But the point is, when your brother finds out I've gone on a vacation with you, he'll give up any idea he had about marriage to me."

"Why is that?" His voice had taken on a darker tone.

Olivia's impulsive nature had once again caused her to leap before she looked.

But this was serious business. The most serious of her existence.

It was Luc she loved with every fiber of her being. The longer he didn't say anything, the more she realized that if she didn't give him the right answer, she might just lose him forever....

Dear Reader,

I came from a family of five sisters and one brother. The four oldest girls were my parents' first family. There was a space before my baby sister and baby brother came along.

My mother called the first four her little women, and gave each of us a Madame Alexander doll from the *Little Women* series based on the famous book by Louisa May Alcott. We may not have been quadruplets, but we were close in age and definitely felt a connection to each other.

In our early twenties, I recall a time when I took the train from Paris, France, where I'd been studying, to meet one of my sisters at the port in Genoa, Italy, where her ship came in from New York. Some of my choicest memories are our glorious adventures as two blond American sisters on vacation along the French and Italian Rivieras, dodging Mediterranean playboys.

When I conceived THE HUSBAND FUND trilogy for Harlequin Romance®, I have no doubt the idea of triplet sisters coming to Europe on a lark to intentionally meet some gorgeous Riviera playboys sprang to life from my own family experiences at home and abroad.

Meet Greer, Olivia and Piper, three characters drawn from my imagination who probably have traits from all four of my wonderful, intelligent, talented sisters in their makeup.

Enjoy!

Rebecca Winters

Book 3: *To Marry for Duty,* Harlequin Romance #3835, on sale March 2005
www.rebeccawinters-author.com

TO WIN HIS HEART
Rebecca Winters

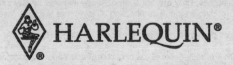

HARLEQUIN®

TORONTO • NEW YORK • LONDON
AMSTERDAM • PARIS • SYDNEY • HAMBURG
STOCKHOLM • ATHENS • TOKYO • MILAN • MADRID
PRAGUE • WARSAW • BUDAPEST • AUCKLAND

ISBN 0-373-03827-5

TO WIN HIS HEART

First North American Publication 2005.

This edition published by arrangement with Harlequin Books S.A.

® and TM are trademarks of the publisher. Trademarks indicated with ® are registered in the United States Patent and Trademark Office, the Canadian Trade Marks Office and in other countries.

www.eHarlequin.com

Printed in U.S.A.

CHAPTER ONE

August 2nd
Monza, Italy

"GOOD night, Cesar. I've had a spectacular time."

After the party downstairs with his Formula I racing team, Cesar walked Olivia to her hotel room, but it irritated her when he looped his arms around her neck outside the door.

Since he never drank before a race, she knew for a fact it couldn't be the effect of alcohol making him amorous all of a sudden.

Twenty-nine-year-old Cesar de Falcon, known as Cesar Villon when he used his paternal grandmother's maiden name Villon to race, was all flash and excitement, the ultimate charmer, albeit one who was still too obsessed with his career to be taken seriously.

Neither during the night of the Monaco Grand Prix in June, or throughout the last two days in Monza prior to tomorrow's race had Olivia led him to believe there was anything but friendship between them. There couldn't be.

She was painfully in love with his elder brother, Lucien de Falcon.

Though that love wasn't reciprocated, it didn't matter. With her emotions involved elsewhere, she couldn't let go with Cesar and kiss him for the sheer fun of being out with one of Europe's most eligible and sought after playboys. Especially not this particular one.

When she'd come to Europe with her sisters in June, the highlight for Olivia had been to watch the Monaco Grand Prix where the legendary Cesar Villon had taken second place.

It was an absolute fluke that Cesar's cousin, Max, had ended up marrying Greer, one of Olivia's sisters, thus throwing their families together under the most unlikely and unexpected circumstances.

Because of her fascination with Formula I racing before meeting Cesar, she'd been thrilled and flattered by the famous driver's eagerness to show her around. How many times in life did one get a chance to see firsthand what went on behind the scenes of the racing world? Especially with someone as well-known?

"I've had an even more wonderful time, *ma belle*. There's no reason why it can't continue now that we're alone."

"Yes, there is." She averted her face in an attempt to prevent him from kissing her. "You have a big race tomorrow and need your beauty sleep."

"Beauty sleep?" He chuckled before brushing his lips against the side of her cheek. "I intend to get some, but not by myself." So saying, he trapped her against the door and kissed her.

Cesar was an attractive man, very persuasive, but she broke away before he could deepen the kiss. The look of surprise on his face let her know few women had ever resisted him.

"You're not going to invite me in?" He gave her that wounded look so typical of Max, her new, all-Italian brother-in-law.

She smiled, needing to handle this with grace and

discretion considering the fact that he was now Greer's cousin-in-law. It wasn't as if she could risk offending him by her rejection, knowing she would never see him again in this lifetime.

"No, *cousin*," she said the word deliberately. "I'm not. I always sleep alone."

"Always?" He looked shocked to the foundations.

"Always."

"Not even with Fred?"

The mention of her ex-boyfriend, the one who'd followed Formula I racing on TV and had gotten her interested in the sport in the first place, made her chuckle. "Especially not Fred."

"But this is unbelievable."

Olivia burst into laughter. She couldn't help it. "My sisters and I were taught to wait for marriage."

"You mean to tell me Greer and Max—"

"Didn't until their wedding night," she finished the sentence for him.

Now it was his turn to laugh. "Then she lied to you."

"No." Olivia shook her head. "I would stake my life on it." When she could see he wasn't convinced she said, "Tell you what. After they're back from their honeymoon, you can ask Max. He'll tell you the truth."

Cesar grinned. "What if you're wrong?"

"I won't be."

"For the sake of argument, let's assume you are," he teased. "We'll make this a bet. If I win—"

"You won't!" she declared in a note of finality.

He was such a tease, it surprised her when he grasped her upper arms. "The German team thinks they're going to win the Italian Grand Prix tomorrow, but by the end of the race *I* will be the one standing at the podium.

"After a race I always spend a week at the family villa in Positano on the Amalfi Coast where I can be alone. This time I'm taking you there with me to celebrate my victory, so be warned."

No, Cesar, I won't be going anywhere with you.

The man had an ego that wouldn't quit. Any other woman would probably jump at the chance to go off alone with him, but Olivia wasn't one of them.

"You would have to be my husband first."

He flashed her a disarming smile. "Then I guess we'll have to pick out a ring while we're in Positano."

"You're full of it, Cesar, but I like you anyway. I'll be rooting for you tomorrow." She raised up on tiptoe and kissed his cheek, then eased out of his arms. "Good night and good luck," she said before escaping to her room for the night.

Though he represented the epitome of most women's desires, he wasn't the man who'd dominated Olivia's every thought after she and her sisters had flown home to New York to get ready for Greer's wedding.

There was only one man's kiss she wanted. She'd worked herself up into a breathless state just waiting to see Luc again at the wedding, but he'd shot her down within the first moments of their meeting.

You may come off the innocent and have Cesar fooled, Olivia, but I see right through you. You're nothing more than what you Americans call a "groupie."

Really...well if I'm a groupie, then that makes you the jealous older brother with what we Americans call a "game" leg. It must be galling to know you wouldn't be able to climb into Cesar's race car, let alone drive it!

Her body still bristled from the ugly words they'd thrown at each other. He'd actually had the audacity to call her a *groupie!*

How dare he liken her to a sycophant, one of a cast of a thousand hopefuls...those grasping, opportunistic women who hung around the track and flung themselves at idols like Cesar who was single, famous and wealthy.

Luc had made her so furious, she'd been glad to take Cesar up on his invitation to watch him race in the Italian Grand Prix. However it had given off the wrong signal to Cesar who now assumed she was his for the taking.

Everything was Luc's fault. Just thinking about their fiery confrontation outside the chapel caused Olivia's heart to thud painfully.

If he hadn't thrown that final insult at her, she wouldn't have done anything so impulsive.

Unlike his brother, Luc didn't need or crave the limelight, a fact that made him much more appealing to her. Though she found his aloofness disturbing, she was also fascinated that he didn't seem to need anyone. He was a man who lit his own fires and moved in an orbit all his own.

According to Cesar, Luc's energy was tied up in his work as a robotics engineer. She found herself wanting to know everything about him, but Cesar had been strangely silent when it came to details about Luc's life, whether professional or personal.

The most she'd learned was that seven months earlier he'd almost lost his leg in the same tragic ski tram accident that had killed his cousin Nic's fiancée.

Olivia already knew from Greer that Luc had never been married.

It certainly wouldn't have been for lack of opportunity. His serious gray eyes beneath black hair and brows were startlingly beautiful and unexpected when contrasted with the olive complexion of his hard-boned features.

She'd only seen him smile once and thought there couldn't be another man as gorgeous, not even Cesar. But after their bitter quarrel, Olivia had given up hope of ever witnessing that rare sight again.

She imagined the pain from his injured leg had something to do with his saturnine disposition. However Olivia suspected his morose moods were the result of problems that went deeper than the physical.

Some woman must have gotten to him… Whoever it was, she'd done a good job of ruining him for anyone else.

The Falcon men were tall, dark and dashing in that irresistible Mediterranean way. If it were Luc's goal, he could be surrounded by stunning beauties all the time. But he obviously had other things on his mind and was too intelligent and self-confident to need constant attention from the opposite sex.

He definitely didn't want Olivia's. She'd never been so hurt, and was still suffering from the wounds. Yet the more she pondered it, the more she refused to accept his biting remarks as final. That jaded, aloof, thirty-three-year-old brother of Cesar's had misjudged her, and she was going to prove it!

Pounding her pillow, she lay her head back down willing sleep to come, afraid it wouldn't.

* * *

"You're not going to see your brother race in the morning?"

Non, Dieu merci.

"I'm afraid not, *maman*. The doctor plans to drain my knee day after tomorrow, so I'm taking it easy until then." Luc was glad to have a legitimate excuse to give his mother. She would pass it on to his father and Cesar.

"Then take care, *mon fils*. I'll be by in a few days to see how you are doing."

"That won't be necessary. I'll come to see you."

If the doctor's prognosis was correct, Luc's leg was in the last stage of healing. After seven ghastly months of pure physical hell, the end was in sight. He only wished he could say the same about his mental torment, but no medical procedure could fix that.

"Talk to you soon, *maman*." He hung up and sat back in the swivel chair of his private study, staring blindly at the monitor screen.

Normally the math required to do his latest project kept his darkest thoughts at bay, but not tonight. An image of Olivia Duchess in his brother's bed made the bile rise in his throat.

He reached for his cell phone and punched one of the digits. After three rings his cousin picked up.

"Luc? I was wondering if it might be you."

"Who else bothers you at this time of night? Were you in bed?"

"No. I'm in my library working on this blasted manuscript."

"I was just going to ask how it was progressing. Now I won't."

Nic had been going through his own personal hell since Nina's death. On top of his grief that the accident had happened, he was suffering guilt. All because he'd broken his engagement to her an hour before she'd taken that last tram ride up the mountain without him.

Luc would never know if Nic had discovered she'd been unfaithful to his cousin, and that's why he'd called the wedding off. As close as Luc and Nic were, his cousin had never once hinted that Nina had been seeing another man.

But Luc knew she had.

By chance he'd decided to take one more ski run late that day. When he'd gone outside the lodge to get his skis, he'd witnessed a sight that had torn him apart.

Over in the trees he'd seen a stranger with thick, dark blond hair kissing Nina. She gave him her full cooperation before she broke away and hurried toward the tram with her skis.

Having always loved Nic like a brother, Luc intended to confront her and followed her onto the tram. But before he had a chance to take her aside, tragedy struck, killing her and injuring him.

During the long talks at the hospital while Luc underwent several surgeries, Nic finally admitted that he'd never been in love with Nina the way he should have been. He'd agreed to the engagement because of pressure from his parents, particularly his father, who'd wanted the marriage to take place.

But as Nic explained, once the wedding date was set, he realized he couldn't marry her.

His confession hadn't surprised Luc or Max. Nic had never acted like a man madly in love. But since Nic had never breathed a word about Nina's betrayal,

Luc decided his cousin hadn't known anything about it.

After discussing it with Max, the two of them thought it best Nic be kept in the dark since it wouldn't have served any purpose. Nina was dead. Why make it any uglier.

In Luc's mind, whether you were engaged or married, it was adultery if your partner proved to be unfaithful. Luc knew firsthand what it felt like to be betrayed, by his own brother no less. He wouldn't wish the feeling on his worst enemy, let alone Nic of all people.

Thousands of spectators screamed and jumped around when the announcement came over the loud speaker in four different languages that Cesar Villon, the brilliant Formula I race car driver representing Monaco, had claimed the coveted first place at Monza.

Olivia had come to the stands early to watch the race. Now she was on her feet, clapping and cheering like so many of his other fans.

The two days before his race had been an instructive time for her as she'd watched him go through the testing and qualifying trials prior to the big event that he'd just conquered.

Being the fierce competitor he was, he'd made his own prophecy come true. Hopefully he'd forgotten what he'd said about taking her away afterward. But in case he hadn't, she decided to leave Monza so she wouldn't be around for him to collect later in the day, giving him another wrong impression.

Blessed with many gifts, including the fact that he was the younger son of the Duc de Falcon of Monaco, he could be excused for assuming no woman was immune to him. If there were depths to him not yet visible, only time would tell, probably after he was too old to compete anymore.

Half Italian, half Monegasque, Cesar's movie star looks made him the supreme favorite with the crowd. Filled with the matchless optimism of a man who knows he's number one, he'd arranged for Olivia to sit near the podium. But she didn't try to reach him after the ceremony was over. Even if she'd wanted to, it would have been a physical impossibility.

Not only was he basking in the adulation of thousands of screaming fans while he drank champagne and pressed his lips to the winner's cup—at least a dozen gorgeous female admirers were now crowding him, hanging on his arm, lifting their mouths for his kiss which he passed around with obvious relish.

Naturally the spectacle provided hundreds of photo ops for the many international journalists covering the race. By tomorrow morning pictures of him embracing one beauty after another would grace the front page of a thousand newspapers and magazine covers.

For Olivia, the whole scene was a huge turnoff. Her sense of distaste for such a lifestyle deepened as she watched the women battling for position, hoping to be the one he took home for the night. Little did they know that last night Olivia had been his target.

Scenes like the one going on in front of her right now happened to Cesar before and after every race. Women would continue to swarm around him like bees, and he would respond for as long as racing fever was in his blood.

Olivia recognized that any woman unfortunate enough to fall in love with an international sports celebrity would have to put up with a mistress more merciless than any flesh-and-blood female.

While she stood there staring blindly in Cesar's direction, the idea that had taken root in her mind last night had turned into a fully fledged plan. She couldn't leave the grandstand fast enough to put it into action.

Without hesitation she worked her way through the crowds to reach the cue of taxis outside the race track. "The Accademia Hotel," she told the driver.

"Si, signorina."

Once back in her room, she would phone her sister Piper, who was already in Genoa, Italy, on business.

Some mockups of their calendars in Italian were ready for them to examine. If they thought the finished products looked good, she'd run off a bunch for Signore Tozetti to distribute in the Parma region. Provided they sold well, it could mean a lot more orders down the road.

Olivia was supposed to be there to help make the decision before they flew home to New York together. But she'd changed her mind about leaving Europe just yet, and she trusted Piper's judgment completely.

Her sister wouldn't approve of Olivia's plan to go after Luc. Neither would Greer. Luckily she wasn't around to quash Olivia's idea. Thanks to Maximilliano di Varano, the love of Greer's life, Greer was on her honeymoon.

It had taken a very special man to break up the Duchess triplets, three blond sisters who caused a minor sensation at birth and bore a strong resemblance to each other without being identical.

Max had taken one look at Greer with her amethyst

eyes, and the dedicated bachelor had fallen so hard, Olivia knew he would never recover.

Since their nuptials four days ago in the private chapel of the Varano family palace in Parma, the two lovers had been honeymooning at an intimate hide-away somewhere in Greece.

The look of desire and adoration in Max's eyes after kissing his bride at the altar revealed to the whole world how he felt about Greer. There was no telling how long he planned to keep her to himself, but Olivia had a hunch it would be at least a month before she and Piper heard from their sister. Long enough for Olivia to follow through with her daring scheme…

With Greer married off, Olivia's world had changed. She was feeling a heady new sense of free-dom both physical and psychological. She figured Piper was enjoying the freedom, too. Without Greer around to tell them how to think and what they were going to do next, Olivia could finally be master of her own destiny.

It wasn't that she didn't love Greer. On the con-trary, she adored her. Still, it was a relief not to have to face her and hear her say, *I told you it would be a mistake to go off with Cesar. If you do that, then you're the kind of stupid, naive, dumb blond he se-duces after every race.*

Despite the fact that Luc's antipathy toward Olivia had made her do it, heat filled Olivia's cheeks to re-alize that once Greer had left on her honeymoon, Olivia had gone off and done the exact, stupid thing Greer had warned her not to do.

In fact it was Greer who'd told Olivia she wasn't in love with Fred. Olivia had already figured that out after meeting Luc, but she'd gone on dating Fred for the six weeks prior to Greer's wedding in an effort to forget Luc and prove that Greer's power over her wasn't absolute.

Unfortunately she'd paid for it in the end when she'd been forced to tell Fred that it was really over. She'd been very unfair to him by leading him on, and was still smarting from the pain she'd caused him. One piercing glance from Greer with that ''I told you so, now you've really done it'' look, hadn't helped matters.

What really miffed Olivia was the fact that even though Max had claimed Greer for his wife and taken her away, Olivia was still battling her sister's powerful influence over her. She could just imagine Greer's reaction if she knew what Olivia was planning now.

You're what? Are you insane? Didn't we all learn a very important lesson the first time around?

''*Signorina?*'' the driver called over his shoulder. They'd arrived at the hotel. She'd been so immersed in her new strategy, she hadn't even noticed!

After paying him a bundle of Euros she didn't even bother to count, she got out of the taxi and rushed inside, anxious to set things in motion.

Once she'd confirmed tickets on a flight to Nice leaving in two hours, she phoned Piper at her hotel in Genoa.

After relating the spectacular news that Cesar had won the Italian Grand Prix, Olivia told Piper what she was intending to do.

''You're *what?*'' Her sister sounded suspiciously like Greer just then, which didn't help matters.

"I'm going back to Monaco to force Luc to make my trip good. It's payback time."

"Say that again?"

"You heard me," Olivia answered defiantly. "We were cheated out of our first trip to Europe because Max and his cousins thought we were jewel thieves and they ruined everything!

"By the time the whole business got straightened out, our vacation had to be aborted because Max wanted to be alone with Greer on the *Piccione*. Luc owes me ten days on that boat!"

"It's Fabio Moretti's boat! August is still high season. Some other tourists have probably chartered it. Don't forget it's the Moretti's livelihood."

"I'm sure Luc will be able to work something out with Fabio. We paid three thousand dollars each for a trip along the Riviera that never happened!"

"Technically you're right, Olivia. But in return we acquired Max, the dream brother-in-law who has treated us like the Duchess of Parma herself while we stayed at his family's royal palace. That beats any vacation I can think of.

"Besides, what are you complaining about? Your dream came true when Cesar whisked you off to Monza for the last three days. I thought you were crazy about *him*. At least that's what you told Fred."

Conscience made Olivia bite her lip. "I had to tell Fred something that would help him retain his pride. If I'd been truthful and said I couldn't picture him as my husband, it would have hurt him a lot more."

"Okay... I can buy that, but what about Cesar?"

"He's a friend. Even if he weren't, he's spoken for."

"By whom?"

"By the entire female population of Europe!"

"Yeah, well Greer already told you that."

Olivia ground her teeth. "Greer doesn't know everything."

"Yes, she does."

"She didn't know we talked Daddy into setting up that phony Husband Fund that brought us to Europe in the first place."

After a moment of quiet, "That's true. It's probably the only secret we ever kept from her."

"Yup. And it worked!" A satisfied smile broke out on Olivia's face. "We finally got her married off. Now we can do what we want, and I want to go on the vacation that never happened. Don't you?"

"Maybe one day. At the moment we've got a calendar business to run."

"Has Signore Tozzeti decided if he wants to take us on as a client?"

"Not yet. He says there are a few other people in his company he needs to talk to, but they're on vacation, so he won't be able to get back to us for a while."

"Great."

"That's why we've got to go home and see about enlarging the market there. Otherwise we're not going to be able to pay the rent. We need to do it now!"

"You sound just like Greer!"

Greer was the oldest triplet by a matter of minutes. Yet Olivia, who'd been born last with Piper in the middle, had always been dominated by Greer, their natural born leader.

Over the years she *had* made the decisions about everything, whether Olivia or Piper liked them or not.

For the first time ever, Olivia could do what she wanted without having to hear Greer's opinion.

"With Greer gone, someone needs to talk sense into you. What's the *real* reason you want to stay? You and Luc looked like mortal enemies after the wedding ceremony, so I don't understand why you would dare confront him again—oh, no—tell me it isn't true."

"What?"

"Tell me you haven't fallen for Luc de Falcon—"

Her cheeks turned to flame.

"Olivia? You *can't!*"

"What do you mean, I can't?"

"Because you just can't, that's all."

"Why?"

"Think of Greer."

"That's all I've ever done. We've had to do everything her way because she always took charge. Now she's married, I want to think about *moi* for a change."

"Then you need to think again because Luc is Max's first cousin."

"So?"

"So, Greer married Max, and Luc has become her family, too. You can't horn in!"

"Excuse me?"

"Look, Olivia. She's found her heart's desire in Max. This is her world, her turf. We need to leave well enough alone."

"It's a free country," she retorted.

"No, it's not, and you know exactly what I mean." Olivia did know, but she didn't like Piper reminding her. "Greer needs time to make a new life with Max.

He married a triplet, and don't think he isn't worried about it!

"At the wedding feast he didn't make that crack about the three of us being joined at the hip, heart and brain for nothing. We have to help Greer cut the apron strings, which means we need to back off and give our sister her space."

"Luc lives in Monaco, not Colorno, Italy."

"That's not the point. The cousins are super close. Besides, it just wouldn't work for you to get involved with Luc, even if he were interested, which he…isn't."

The slight hesitation before the last word set off alarm bells inside Olivia. "How do you know?"

"Because…I just do."

"What do you know that I don't?" she fired.

"More than you want to hear."

She blinked. "How come?"

"Because it might hurt you."

Hurt? "You mean you're not going to tell me?"

"No. I promised someone I wouldn't," Piper's voice trailed.

"I see." She slid off the side of the bed and stood up. "Well in that case I plan to proceed as if you hadn't warned me. With a little hard work I'll make him change his mind."

"You'll be playing with fire."

"Then that's my problem isn't it."

"Don't snap at me, Olivia. I know you're feeling as lost without Greer as I am. You simply don't want to admit it."

She tossed her head back. "I admit it feels strange to be two-thirds of a whole. In time I trust we'll both get over it."

"Until we do, please come home with me."

"Not yet, Piper."

"Listen to me. You don't mess with a man like Luc. In more ways than one he's a different breed from anyone you've ever known. Besides, and this is probably the most important point, he has the distinction of being the only male who never fell under your spell. You can't win them all, Olivia. Trust me on this."

"Are you through, *Greer?*"

"That wasn't very nice," Piper came back in a quiet voice.

Olivia clutched the phone tighter. "I'm sorry. It's just that I'm tired of people telling me what to do."

"Translated you mean, Greer and me."

Since the answer was obvious, Olivia didn't say anything.

"Whatever happened to all for one, and one for all?"

"There's no more *all.*" She prided herself on keeping a steady voice.

"You and I have each other. I don't want to see you in any more pain. It's been hard enough on us to lose Daddy."

At the mention of their father who'd died in April, Olivia's eyes smarted. "I don't intend to stay in pain. My plan is foolproof."

There was a long, resigned silence. "What is it exactly you're intending to do?"

"Get him to propose, at which time I will say *yes.*"

"Not that again! Luc already knows about the Husband Fund scheme, so it won't work on him."

"Yes, it will. He thinks I'm interested in Cesar, so

he'll jump at the chance to save his brother from a fate worse than death by taking me on Fabio's boat. While we're basking in the sun, I'll find ways to thaw out his heart until he's unable to resist me. By the time we dock at Vernazza, he'll have proposed.''

"You'll never break him down, Olivia.''

She clutched the phone tighter. "Want to bet?''

After a pause, "I don't bet when I already know the outcome. I repeat. You'll live to regret this.'' Piper's voice sounded like Greer's at her most prophetic. "Come home with me and we'll find you a nice American guy to date.''

"After Fred, no thank you.''

"Not like Fred. Europe doesn't have the monopoly on exciting men.''

"Sounds like you're trying to convince yourself!''

"Don't be ridiculous.''

"I've already met the man I want for my husband, Piper. There's no talking me out of it.''

"You think he's hurt you now...you just wait!''

Olivia refused to let the secret Piper was withholding about Luc get to her. "We'll see.''

"It's your funeral, but whatever happens, call me tomorrow. I have to know where you are and where I can reach you or I won't have any peace. I should be in Kingston by noon at the latest.''

"I promise to phone,'' Olivia vowed. "Have a safe flight. I'm glad Tom will be there to meet you. Be sure he takes a look around the apartment for you first.''

"Don't worry about me.''

Now Olivia was doing what she'd accused Piper of doing—telling her what to do. Running her life. "Okay, I won't. Talk to you later. Love you.''

"Love you, too."

After Olivia hung up, she sat down to write a letter to Cesar. She needed to couch her words carefully.

"Dear cousin-in-law," she began. Once she'd explained that her heart belonged to another, she thanked him profusely for the wonderful time he'd shown her, thanked him for his kindness and generosity and praised him for his latest win.

"May all your wins in the coming years be as successful. I remain your friend and greatest fan from the U.S. Olivia Duchess."

Pleased with her message, she sealed it in the envelope and took it downstairs to leave with the concierge.

"I don't know when Monsieur Villon will come back to the hotel to check out, but as soon as he does, will you make certain he gets this?"

"Si, signorina."

"Grazie."

After paying her bill, she carried her suitcase outside to the limo. The hotel provided transportation to the airport. Hopefully she was leaving soon enough to avoid the mass of tourists who probably wouldn't jam the terminal until tomorrow after a night of nonstop partying.

Once she reached Nice, she would take a taxi to the Falcon Villa in Monaco and surprise Luc. If her plan was going to work, it was imperative she catch him off guard. Forewarned and he might disappear on her. She couldn't let that happen.

CHAPTER TWO

"PLEASE wait for me."

The chauffeur de taxi nodded while Olivia approached the front door of the villa. It was seven-thirty on a hot August evening. She could still feel the heat rising from the street.

A maid answered. She recognized Olivia from her previous visit in June. When Olivia asked if she could see Luc, the other woman explained he didn't live there with his parents, yet Olivia distinctly remembered Luc claiming that he did!

Cross because it had been a deliberate ploy on his part to keep his private life private, she was forced to ask the maid where to find him. She learned he had his own home, the Mas de Falcon. Olivia wasn't familiar with the word.

The maid wrote down the address for her. Olivia thanked her, then gave it to the taxi driver. He nodded and they took off once more, heading for the region above the city.

In a few minutes they drove down a private road that opened up into a charming courtyard filled with pots of flowers. There she discovered an exquisite pale pink, two-story villa with light blue shutters at all the windows. Apparently this was the back of the house.

Like an eagle's eyrie, the *mas* sat perched on a hill overlooking Monaco-Ville. The view would be magnificent.

In front of the garage at the side of the house were two vehicles: a truck that had to be several years old, and a black sports car. Hopefully that meant Luc was home, but she wouldn't know until she rang the doorbell.

Assuming he employed staff who could call another taxi for her in case he wasn't there, she paid the driver, then waved him off.

Determined as she'd ever been in her life, she walked up to the back entrance with her suitcase. "Be home, Luc."

With her heart pounding out of rhythm, she pushed the buzzer and waited. When there was no answer, she rang again.

On the third try, she heard noise like someone swearing. Shivering a little, she was glad she didn't understand French.

Then the door opened to reveal Luc himself, dressed in low-slung cutoff jeans and nothing else. Though she could see scarring on the shin bone of his leg beneath the knee, he looked so blatantly male with the dusting of black hair on his well cut chest and physique, she couldn't think or talk.

In that dizzying moment, she didn't notice that his mouth had formed a white line of anger. Not until her eyes wandered helplessly up his hard-muscled body to his striking face.

"What in the hell are *you* doing here?" Despite the anger in that low, grating voice, she loved his French accent when he spoke English.

"What are you doing answering the door without your cane?" Olivia fired back. She wasn't about to be intimidated by him. "You don't have to prove how macho you are in front of people, especially me. We're family now," she added just to irritate him.

His hands went to his hips, a gesture that emphasized his total masculinity. "Is that your unsubtle way of telling me you and Cesar ran off and got married after the race?"

She laughed. "Wouldn't you hate it if I said yes, thereby proving that I'm the ultimate groupie who was out for everything I could get from your brother, and did!"

His silvery eyes had narrowed to slits. "Why are you here?"

"What?" Her expressive brows lifted in question. "Not even a 'won't you come in and make yourself comfortable'?"

"You're not an invited guest."

"Not even when we're related through marriage?"

He stiffened. "Whatever it is you have to say, make it fast. I'm in a hurry."

"Is that why you were cursing on your way to the door?" she taunted him with relish. "If you don't have the time to be civil to me right now, I'll be happy to wait."

If looks could kill… "Then you'll have a long one because I'm on my way out and don't know when I'll be back."

"That's no problem. I'll go with you and keep you company. As you can see, I brought my suitcase with me so I'm ready to travel."

He rubbed his chest in a motion he probably wasn't aware of. The fact that his first cousin Max was married to her sister was undoubtedly the only reason he hadn't slammed the door in her face yet.

"What's this all about?" Talk about a forbidding tone—

Standing her ground she said, "The trip my sisters and I never went on of course! The trip you and your cousins ruined for us. The trip that cost us over twenty thousand dollars after the bills we incurred by being forced to buy new bikes to try to get away from you.

"Shall I count the ways you destroyed the dream?" Her fingers started to tick everything off. "First, Max had us detained by the police in Genoa the second we got off the plane, then he stalked us while we walked around Portofino.

"After that, he inveigled you and Nic to take over as the crew aboard the *Piccione*. At that point the three of you sabotaged our itinerary, stole the family pendants our parents gave us on our sixteenth birthday, threw us in jail, prevented us from boarding a plane home and then forced us to show up at your family's villa to help draw out the real jewel thief.

"The thief you didn't catch by the way!" she mocked. "All this because you *thought* we'd stolen an identical pendant from the palace, which we didn't!"

Her fists went to her waist, drawing his piercing gaze to the curves beneath the leaf green cotton dress molding her body. "You were totally unfair to us, and now I'm here to collect. Since Max is on his honeymoon, and Nic left for London after the wedding, that leaves *you* to pay up.

"You owe me, Luc! So I've arrived to inform you that you're taking me for a ten-day trip on the *Piccione* before I go back to New York."

He shifted his weight, a sign his leg was probably bothering him. "You make a compelling case, but I don't buy any of it. Why don't you try telling me the truth for a change. What's the real reason you've come to my home on a Sunday night, uninvited? Where's Cesar?''

''I haven't a clue. Well, that's not exactly true. The last time I saw him, he was at the winner's podium kissing one beautiful groupie after another, having the time of his life.''

For just a moment she thought she saw a shadow cross over his face, but maybe it was a light plane passing overhead, hiding the rays of a setting sun for a moment. Then he smirked. ''What's the matter? Couldn't you take the competition?''

''That question doesn't deserve an answer. The truth is, I had other things on my mind. Remember the Husband Fund?''

''What about it?'' he practically snapped.

''I'm afraid I may have hooked the wrong playboy without meaning to, and I need an out.''

''Which playboy would that be? There've been so many.'' His insulting remark was meant to sting. Well, she would sting him back!

''Cesar,'' she admitted.

Luc eyed her with disdain. ''I don't see him anywhere around. Now you'll have to excuse me.'' He started to close the door.

''Last night he said something about buying me an engagement ring after the race.''

She'd purposely slipped in that last tidbit before he could shut her out completely. Olivia was a hundred percent sure Cesar had been joking, but Luc didn't know that.

''I left Monza as soon as it was over and came straight here.''

To her satisfaction she didn't hear the click that would have severed all contact. The door opened wider again. A stillness had stolen over Luc.

"He asked you to marry him?" his voice grated with incredulity.

Her instincts had been right. The idea of her becoming Luc's sister-in-law was so repugnant to him, he was caught in a vise.

"Isn't that what an engagement ring means? Or is your younger brother in the habit of promising one to every groupie he fancies without any intention of delivering…"

He raked a hand through his vibrant black hair, a gesture that indicated the news had disturbed him. Good. She hoped his concern to protect his brother from a predator like herself was great enough to agree to her plan.

"What kind of game are you playing with him?" came the voice of ice.

"Game?" She feigned innocence. "I admit it was exciting to be wined and dined by him for a little while. Fred got me interested in Formula I racing and I followed Cesar's success for a long time before we ever met.

"Meeting your brother was a great thrill. He's a wonderful man, and he's done everything to show me a fantastic time, but—"

"But all along it's been dull, boring Fred you wanted, and now you're afraid to tell Cesar?" She felt his question like the tip of a whip against her skin.

"No," she came back, intrigued to discover he'd remembered an offhand comment she'd made about Fred in his hearing. "I ended it with Fred before I flew here for Greer's wedding."

"How many dead bodies are lying around in that colorful past of yours?" he muttered in an acerbic tone. The wounds were growing.

"My past is none of your business, but Cesar *is*."

A nerve ticked at the corner of his sensual mouth. "Go on!"

"Well…Cesar knows I'm not seeing Fred anymore. So he's not going to believe there's another man in my life, and he would be right. But that's not what I told him in the note I left for him at the hotel in Monza."

"That was like waving a red flag," Luc drawled with contempt.

"I thought I was being polite," Olivia asserted. "After the race I went back to the Accademia in a taxi and dashed off a letter before checking out. It was a combination goodbye–thank you note.

"I left it with the concierge to give to him when he came in. In it I explained that my heart belonged to another, but I wished him success in the future. Since Cesar is aware that other person isn't Fred, I'm afraid I've painted myself into a corner, and now I need help."

Lines marred his features. "You should have thought of that before you went to bed with him."

"The Duchess girls don't sleep around!"

"That's an interesting fairy tale."

She bridled. "Cesar said the same thing, so I told him to ask Max when he gets back from his honeymoon if he doesn't believe me. Theirs was a *white* wedding. Why do you think they got married so fast?"

He folded his arms. "Why are you digressing? If I'm to be of assistance to you, you have to tell me exactly how far things have progressed between you two. The truth this time.''

"You won't believe me if I tell you, so why should I bother.''

"You're still avoiding answering my question,'' Luc reminded her testily. "I can assure I'm not asking out of a prurient desire to know the intimate details, just the facts. But if you don't want my help after all…'' He was a breath away from shutting the door on her.

She had to tamp down her euphoria. Obviously the thought of his brother marrying her disgusted him enough to listen.

"After the way you spoke to me at the wedding, do you honestly think I would darken your doorstep if I didn't?'' she challenged.

A war was waging inside him. She knew it by the tautness of his Gallic features. "I repeat. How far did you go to accomplish what no other groupie has managed to do?'' he persisted.

"I didn't have to do anything. He's the one who kissed me outside my hotel room before I told him I had to go in.''

"And you expect me to believe he did *all* the work?''

Her brows knit together. "Why do you have to know that?''

"So you *did* respond,'' he muttered, "which means he'll believe you were being a provocative tease.''

She gave him a vexed look. "I couldn't help but respond a little bit. Your brother's the stuff a woman's dreams are made of. But the truth is, I have no interest in being his wife. For one thing, he won't make a good husband until his racing days are over. I've a feeling that day won't come for years yet.''

"So you're still spouse hunting in Riviera waters?''

"I would be if you and your cousins hadn't robbed us of our trip! It's only fair you make up for it now. Who knows? I might meet an exciting playboy with husband potential while I'm waterskiing or exploring some island.

"The point is, when Cesar finds out I've gone on a vacation with you, he'll give up any idea he had about marriage to me.''

"Why is that?'' His voice had taken on a darker tone.

"You don't know?''

His face closed up. "I wouldn't have asked otherwise.''

"Since the first time I met Cesar, I've discovered you're the only man in the world who intimidates him. You're kind of like Greer incarnate.'' Luc's black brows furrowed. "You know—the *oldest* one in the family. The one who rules by divine right?''

"No, I didn't know.'' He looked like thunder.

"Well you wouldn't! You don't have to. You were just born in charge. The one who knows everything, even if you don't!'' She paused to catch her breath.

"Anyway, Cesar will think you must be the man who stole my heart after I came to the Riviera the first time. He wouldn't dare come after me knowing I was under your protection, so to speak.''

Like the day she and her sisters dove off the *Piccione* into the warm blue water of the Mediterranean to get away from Luc and his cousins, Olivia's impulsive nature had once again caused her to leap before she looked.

But this was serious business. The most serious of her existence.

It was Luc she loved with every fiber of her being. The longer he didn't say anything, the more she realized that if he didn't give her the right answer, she would be in permanent mourning.

His eyes looked dark in the fading light. "Nothing's sacred to a woman like you, is it." A woman like me? "Haven't you realized by now you can't play at life without paying too great a price?"

Those words were meant to debilitate her. They reminded her of Piper's warning on the phone earlier in the day that Luc could hurt her if she let him.

She struggled for breath. "My parents raised my sisters and me to believe fairy tales do come true. I can't help it if they were divinely happy and everything worked out for them.

"You have to admit the Husband Fund they set up managed to get Greer and Max together. I've never seen a more besotted couple."

"You're straying from the point again. It's a bad tendency of yours."

"No stronger than your tendency to ridicule everything," she fired back. "Can you think of a better way to put your brother off so he gets the message without causing damage? He *is* Greer's cousin-in-law through marriage. So are you of course.

"I don't want to be the one responsible for some kind of rift in our families before they've even come home from their honeymoon."

"You should have thought of that before you leaped into Cesar's Ferrari."

"You would have leaped too if you'd never been in one before. How many people will ever get the opportunity to drive in such a car with a world-class Formula I race car pro like your brother? It's an experience not to be missed. But I'm forgetting this is a sensitive issue for you since you can't drive."

His eyes glittered dangerously.

"The sooner you phone Fabio Moretti and tell him I'm ready to go on my trip now, the trip you stole from me, the sooner we can leave Monaco where Cesar won't be able to find me."

Luc gave a careless shrug of his broad shoulders. "I'm afraid a trip for me is out of the question. I'm due at the hospital in the morning for a procedure on my knee. For the next week I'll have to stay off it except to do some exercises and water therapy."

"Perfect!" she blurted excitedly. "The *Piccione* is pure luxury. You can recuperate on it at your leisure while I enjoy myself. The first mate also acts as steward, so he can wait on you. Call Fabio right now! Tell him I want the same itinerary Greer planned for us before."

"He'll be booked solid for August," Luc declared as if the final word had been spoken. But Olivia wasn't about to let him wriggle out of this.

"Even if he is, there are accommodations for six guests aboard the catamaran. Probably not all the bedrooms are taken. If you don't want to phone him and arrange it, I will. He *knows* you owe me, and he won't turn me down." After a slight pause, "Even if Cesar wanted to come after me, he wouldn't relish being confined with a boatload of tourists in such close quarters."

She'd thrown out that last salvo for leverage, but nothing seemed to be working. Just when she thought they'd reached gridlock, he surprised her by wheeling around to reach for his cane lying in the middle of the foyer. He must have tripped on it answering the door, which would account for his cursing earlier.

Though he didn't ask her to follow him, she assumed he wouldn't have left the door open if he'd expected her to remain on the porch.

Consumed by curiosity to see his home, she trailed after him with her suitcase, noticing his limp was barely noticeable anymore. The minute she stepped over the threshold, she was enchanted.

This was *real* French country with a mix of period furniture. The authentic kind of fabulous treasures belonging to a man with a royal heritage.

Alcoves, beamed ceilings, inlaid parquet floors, hand-carved furniture, flowers in copper pots, wrought iron fixtures, books, paintings. Sheer elegance that could only be created and enjoyed by someone of Luc's aristocratic status.

Once again Olivia was reminded that Luc's father was a duc, and his mother a Varano who was one of the direct descendents of the House of Parma-Bourbon in Italy.

Greer was now married to Max, the son of the Duc of Parma-Bourbon. After their honeymoon, she would be living with her husband in Colorno, a town near Parma, in an Italian villa so fantastic, words failed Olivia.

They failed her now. She looked around in wonder as they passed through to a study off the entrance hall where a stairway of hand-painted Provence tiles rose in a graceful curve to the second floor.

Surely Luc employed staff to keep the villa in such perfect condition, but she could see no sign of them right now.

After being in the hot sun most of the day, his house felt blessedly cool to Olivia. Since he was ignoring her, she entered his inner sanctum without being asked, and sank down in one of two fat Louis XV chairs upholstered in a fabric with the Falcon crest.

Luc moved around his huge oak desk with an ancient porcelain clock placed on top. What a striking contrast to see the master of this small palace of a villa dressed in nothing more than a pair of well-worn cutoffs.

Still standing, he reached for the house phone. Before long she heard him say, "*Ciao,* Fabio." The next thing she knew he was speaking fluent Italian.

The multilingual Varano cousins were close as brothers and exceptional men in their own right. More than ever Olivia was determined to get Luc to fall in love with her. She was so crazy about him she would do whatever it took.

Olivia wasn't under any delusion that Luc wanted to be with her. On the contrary. The fact that he was trying to arrange a trip with Fabio only proved he would do anything to save Cesar from her clutches.

The situation couldn't be working out better.

Please make it happen, Fabio.

"I wish I could accommodate you, Luc, but the boat is fully chartered for August. There's one bedroom left for you if you were to join us in Monterosso on Tuesday. Signorina Duchess could use it until Saturday. You could have my berth in the crew's quarters and I could sleep on deck."

"You're a good friend, Fabio, but I would never ask such a favor of you."

While they were talking, Luc kept his eye on

Olivia, wondering what in the devil she was really up to. He'd learned not to trust one word that came out of that treacherously beautiful mouth of hers. However he didn't believe that even *she* would lie about Cesar's intention to give her an engagement ring.

Life hadn't been the same since the Duchess triplets had exploded into Luc's world with the force of a colliding meteor. They'd done the unexpected at every turn, driving him and his cousins crazy.

But because Cesar had entered into this latest equation, Luc had been hesitant to shut the door on her half an hour ago and leave her to her own cunning devices.

"I wish I could help you," Fabio murmured, "but the other charter companies in the Cinq Terre region are as busy as I am. If I had more time, and you didn't need a luxury craft, I could probably arrange something for you."

A luxury craft...

Luc's thoughts shot ahead. "What about your friend, Giovanni? Does he still have that old sailboat?"

"Of course, but it needs a paint and has no sail at the moment."

That was even better. "Would he let me use it? I'll pay him what the Duchess triplets paid you."

"You mean just to putt around Vernazza's bay while you do a little fishing? You must be joking! Twelve thousand dollars is more money than he makes in five months at the trattoria in Vernazza.

"He'll be overjoyed to let you borrow it for as long as you want, but I seriously doubt Signorina Duchess will step foot on it. She paid for a luxury boat to take her as far as the Spanish Riviera, and she expects a crew to wait on her.''

A diabolical smile broke the corners of Luc's mouth. When she found out she was the designated crew who had to do all the work, that spoiled, mercenary, scheming female would leave Vernazza on the first train out of there.

If Cesar wanted her so much, he'd have to go after her. As for Luc, she'd be out of his life forever. By tomorrow afternoon, he'd be liberated. In a week he'd be able to drive a car again, and life would get back to normal as he knew it before the advent of the Duchess sisters.

It didn't matter that his skiing days were over. The alpine sport he'd enjoyed from childhood was now a thing of the past. But because of modern medical science, he'd be able to walk again without the assistance of a cane. When the week was up, he'd celebrate by burning it.

''Luc? Are you still there?''

''Forgive me, Fabio. I was distracted for a moment. To answer your question, Signorina Duchess won't have a choice if she wants to get in a Mediterranean trip before she flies back to New York. If you'll give me Giovanni's phone number, I'll call him and see if he's willing to let me use it starting tomorrow. I know this is short notice.''

''No problem. *I'll* take care of everything, Luc. You can consider it a fait accompli. The *Gabbiano* will be waiting for you at the Vernazza dock.''

''Excellent. *Grazie,* Fabio. *Ciao.*'' Mademoiselle Olivier was in for the surprise of her life!

The second he hung up, his gaze locked with a pair of flame-blue eyes.

"Well?" she prodded. "What did Signore Moretti have to say?"

"He told me to tell you that for the Duchess of Kingston, he would move heaven and earth to accommodate you."

"I knew Fabio would pull through! But the next time you talk to him, tell him I like heaven and earth right where they are. All I'm asking is to go on the vacation Daddy paid for."

Ah yes. The famous Husband Fund. Who could forget? It proved that truth *was* stranger than fiction.

According to Max, the Duchess sisters had come to Europe the first time around on the money their father had willed to them, money he called the "Husband Fund." They could only use it to try to snag a husband.

Absurd and ridiculous as the plan had sounded, it had worked. Greer Duchess was now Signora di Varano, with Max her blissful groom.

Both Luc and Nic had been stunned by the way their cousin had run to his own wedding with such eagerness. In fact he'd gotten engaged to Greer four days after meeting her, which had to be some kind of record.

Luc studied her for a moment. "It seems you're going to get your wish. The boat will be ready for us tomorrow."

"But you said you have to go to the hospital in the morning. Won't you need a day of rest first?"

What was she playing at now, feigning concern. "I thought the main point of this exercise was to remove you from Cesar's grasp as soon as possible."

"Well of course it is, but not at the expense of your leg."

"I had no idea you cared."

From their first meeting, Olivia had seemed to take particular delight in mocking him over anything to do with his injury. Her last taunt about his not being able to get in Cesar's race car, let alone drive it, still rankled. Being prohibited from driving for the last seven months had served as its own prison.

"Of course I care," she blurted. "You *are* a human being, even if you don't display the normal set of emotions. Cesar told me you were into robotics engineering. How very *apropos*."

"I'm glad we understand each other."

She eyed him suspiciously. "Why?"

"You're going to have to fetch and carry for me."

"The *Piccione* is a luxury boat. The crew will help you. I'll be too busy swimming."

"You mean fishing for men."

"That's right. I understand from Cesar that the Prince of Monaco is scuba diving off the coast of Ischia at the moment. His mother was an American. We would have a lot in common. I'm going to tell the captain to set sail for Ischia as soon as we leave port."

"You do that."

"I will!" She tossed her head before wandering over to the window to look out at the view. The gesture brought attention to her cap of gleaming gold curls which was a new hairstyle for her. Over six weeks ago when they'd first met, she'd been wearing it longer.

Short like this, it brought out the classic mold of her facial features. Her eyes looked larger than ever. Luc found himself looking forward to tomorrow when she discovered that she and the steward were one in the same person.

It was hard to believe that only an hour ago Luc had assumed his younger brother had already whisked her off to the Amalfi Coast where the family had a small villa above Positano. It sat high on a cliff overlooking the Mediterranean, one of Cesar's favorite haunts to take his flavor of the month.

When Luc thought of Olivia standing near the altar in some filmy white bridesmaid concoction where she'd caught the golden light from the stained glass windows pouring into the chapel, the image of luscious, succulent golden peaches in rich crème came to mind.

Definitely an enticing taste treat. Cesar could be forgiven for not being able to take his eyes off her during the ceremony.

Since Luc had been the one to introduce her to his brother, he shouldn't have been surprised she would take one look at Cesar and go after him with a vengeance. The ultimate playboy with a title. Just what she'd come to Europe for.

Watching a laughing Olivia drive away from the Varano estate in the Ferrari with Cesar after the wedding was a case in point.

Now she was pretending to run away from his brother, but it was a ploy to sink her hooks deeper until he was caught. Unfortunately she'd come to the wrong man for help. No way was Luc going to allow a treacherous opportunist like Olivia Duchess to succeed at her game, even if she and Cesar deserved each other...

Suddenly she wheeled around. "I don't suppose there'll be a *real* French chef on board this time."

Luc pretended to look in his desk drawer for something. "Fabio employs various locals. I didn't think to ask him which one. You should have taken advantage of my cooking when you had the chance."

"Give me a break. I found out it was your parents' chef who prepared the food before it was brought aboard the *Piccione*."

He darted her a quick glance. "I concede to that happening on one occasion because I was otherwise occupied."

"You mean you and your cousins were too busy playing undercover cop. How come you haven't found your thief yet?"

"Give us a little more time and we will."

Earlier in the day Nic had called Luc, asking him to fly to England. The police had stumbled across a new lead in the case of the family's missing jewelry collection from the Colorno palace in Italy. One of the pieces had turned up at an auction in London. Nic wanted to discuss the new development with him.

Luc had been forced to turn him down because of his hospital visit in the morning, but after his week of recuperation was up, he promised to join Nic in Marbella, Spain, where he lived and they'd discuss new ideas to track down the culprits.

The disappointment in his cousin's voice was understandable. Luc suspected his cousin was looking for an excuse to get together because, like Luc, he was feeling deserted now that the wedding was over. Their cousin Max, who'd been a best friend and brother to them, was now a married man.

"Luc? In case you hadn't noticed, your phone's ringing. From the sound of it, they're not going to hang up. I would imagine it's Cesar looking for me.

''The maid at your parents' house had to give me your address and probably told him I was here. Maybe I should answer it. That way he'll believe you're the man I was referring to in my note. What do you think?''

Luc didn't have to think. She obviously had Cesar eating out of her hand. ''Be my guest.''

CHAPTER THREE

FULL of confidence, Olivia took the receiver Luc handed to her and said hello. When there was no answer she said hello again, a little louder this time. If it was Cesar on the other end, no doubt he was debating whether to hang up or not.

Suddenly a familiar female voice came over the wires. "Olivia Duchess!"

Oh, no. It was *Greer!*

"I didn't want to believe what Piper told me," her sister started in without preamble. "What in heaven's name are you doing at Luc's house, let alone answering his phone? I can't believe you actually followed through with this outrageous plan of yours!"

Olivia spun around so her back faced Luc. She couldn't fathom that her sister was calling all the way from Greece when she was supposed to be in Max's arms right now. Greer could ruin everything!

Think fast, Olivia. "Are you still in Monza?"

"Monza— Oh, I get it. Luc's standing right there next to you. Piper told me about this crazy scheme of yours and begged me to stop you, but I can see it's already too late."

"I'm afraid it is."

"Listen to me—there's something you need to know about Luc. I was hoping I would never have to tell you, but after Piper's emergency phone call, I've decided it's necessary."

"There's nothing else to be said. Please understand. Besides this isn't the time with Luc going into the hospital first thing in the morning for surgery on his leg. It's time for bed right now and he needs a good night's sleep.''

''What surgery? Luc never told Max about that!''

''Luc assures me it's nothing serious, but he won't want visitors for a while. In the meantime, I'm going to nurse him while he recuperates. When he's feeling better the two of you can talk.''

''Olivia Duchess—don't you dare hang up on me! I haven't finished with yo—''

''Congratulations again on your win. You were fabulous. No doubt the German team has left Italy to re-strategize for the next Grand Prix on the schedule. But between you and me they don't stand a chance against you. I'm proud to know you.''

''*Oliviaaaaaaaaaaaaa?*''

''I'll tell him. Good night.''

She turned around and put the receiver back on the hook too fast for Luc to hear her sister's alarmed cry. When she looked up, their eyes collided.

His merciless gaze unnerved her. ''Tell me what?'' he demanded.

''Cesar's worried about your leg and hopes the operation goes well.''

''It's not as much an operation as a procedure done under a local anesthetic.''

She gave a feminine shrug of her shoulders. ''The important thing is, I think I put him off. He's concerned about you, and he isn't going to come charging after me.''

''You expect me to believe that?'' he asked in an urbane voice, but she felt his underlying contempt. ''You kissed him back, remember?''

"At least a dozen women did the same thing to him today after his big win. I don't know how he keeps his girlfriends straight in his mind. The point is, if he does show up, it probably won't be before tomorrow. We'll be long gone from the hospital by then.

"However should he come looking me, I'll tell him that the pity I felt for you on the *Piccione* turned to love, but that I didn't realize it until I went to Monza with him and he started kissing me."

"He'll never buy it." His words dropped like rocks.

"You mean because he knows you're not in love with *me?*" she fired. "Well if everyone didn't know it before the wedding, you made certain they figured it out by the time it was over!

"But it doesn't matter how you feel about me. All that's important is that Cesar realizes I'm here and that I've made my choice, so ther—"

The phone rang again. She grabbed for it, fearing Greer was calling her back, but Luc's hand was faster on the receiver. His smile was wicked as he picked up the receiver.

"*Allo?*" she heard him say. She held her breath, fearing the worst. "*Bonsoir,* Cesar."

Oh, no. Cesar! This was turning into a nightmare.

"Congratulations on another brilliant win." He'd switched to English. Olivia stood stock still, waiting for the bomb to drop. "She's right here."

With a penetrating glance that kept her rooted to the spot, Luc handed her the phone. "You'll have to do a better job of getting rid of him this time around," he whispered. "He's not the grand champion of Formula I racing for nothing."

Feeling as if she was walking on the edge of a cliff that was about to give way at any moment, she put the receiver to her ear. "What is it, Cesar?"

"*Eh bien,* what a greeting! You really do know how to wound. It wasn't until a few minutes ago that I learned you'd been to our parents' house asking to see Luc.

"I expected you to come to the podium after the race today. With so much going on, it was several hours before I could get away to meet you at the hotel. When I did, all I found was your note."

"I really am sorry."

"Now I discover you at my brother's house— Tell me, *ma belle.* What does he have that I don't?"

For once she couldn't figure out if it was his male pride talking, or if he truly had feelings for her.

"Can't we leave it alone and just be friends?"

"So it was love at first sight for you when you met him in June?"

"Yes." She could answer that question honestly.

There was a long silence on his end. "He's a lucky man. By the time I see you again, I hope to God he has realized it." There was a distinct tremor in his voice. "*A bientôt, cherie.*"

Another solemn warning about Luc, this time from a different Cesar than the one he presented to the world. She'd heard real pain underlying his words. What on earth?

Piper hadn't been kidding when she'd said she knew a terrible secret and Olivia sensed that it was to do with Luc, not her. Greer had tried to tell Olivia, but she'd refused to listen.

Luc took the phone from her hand. "You'd better

sit down. You've gone a little pale. It appears my brother is having trouble accepting your rejection."

"I'm all right, however I have to admit he did sound a little shaken." But it was because of *you*, Luc. Not me…

"How soon will he be arriving?"

She bit her lip. "What does *a bientôt* mean?"

Lines darkened his features. "See you soon. Coming from Cesar, it probably means tomorrow."

She swallowed hard, not wanting anything to interfere with her plan. "What time do you have to show up at outpatient in the morning?"

"Six-thirty a.m. The doctor explained it should take about twenty minutes. If all goes well, I should be released by eight-thirty at the latest. I'll arrange for the helicopter to fly us from the hospital to Vernazza."

"That'll be perfect." Perfect. Cesar didn't know anything about the operation. If by any chance he did decide to pay a visit to Luc's home, the two of them would be long gone.

"You're sure you want to disappear on him?" came the sinuous voice.

"Of course!" She turned aside so Luc couldn't tell how excited she was about going away with him. "A clean break is better. I've already said everything I wanted to say in the note I left for him."

Needing to maintain the lie that Cesar was the person who'd phoned twice she added, "I just wish I hadn't told him about your operation. Do you think he'll come to the hospital?"

"Isn't that exactly what you were hoping for?" Luc's expression was grim.

Her chin lifted defiantly. "Think what you want."

"It's not what *I* think." His wintry smile cut to the quick. "It's my brother who thinks he's in love with you."

"He couldn't be! As Greer would say, he's just in the first throes of lust."

Caustic laughter erupted from Luc, but she ignored him. Her thoughts were on her conversation with Cesar who'd emitted strong emotion while they'd been discussing Luc.

Piper knew a secret about Luc, and had been concerned enough to call Greer. For Piper to bother their sister while she was on her honeymoon meant the situation was more serious than Olivia had thought. She needed to have a long talk with Piper without Luc being anywhere around.

She faced him once more. "If you'll phone for a taxi, I'll stay in town tonight and meet you at the hospital in the morning."

"So you can join him at prearranged location?" His eyes glittered dangerously. "I'm afraid not. With five bedrooms upstairs, there's no need for you to go anywhere. In fact I insist you stay so you can help me pack for our trip. My staff isn't here on weekends."

The thought of remaining at the *mas* with him made her almost sick with excitement. She could always call Piper from an upstairs phone after she'd gone to bed.

Olivia eyed him speculatively. "It shouldn't take long. You're not going to need many clothes if you're just going to be lying around in the sun. A few shirts, a couple of pairs of cutoffs like you're wearing, plus a swimsuit for your water therapy ought to be plenty.

Come to think of it, I packed very little for the wedding myself.''

She'd only brought one pair of shorts and her bathing suit for swimming in Max's pool. It would do for starters. When the *Piccione* put into port at various towns, she could go ashore and pick up some more casual clothes so she would look beautiful for Luc.

''A woman who travels light is worth her weight in gold.''

''Why do men always say that?''

''Do I really need to explain why a man would rather see a woman in less than more?''

Wasn't it Max who'd told Greer he lived for the moment when she appeared to him au naturel, like Venus Rising From the Sea?

Olivia would give anything to know if Luc ever had fantasies like that about her, even if he did despise her.

''Funny about that. A woman would rather see a man in uniform.''

''You mean like Fred, your military man? Apparently he didn't look that good in his after all,'' he inserted silkily.

''He looked terrific, but on a scale of one to ten, ten being irresistible, he rated a three.''

''What scale is this?''

''The one my sisters and I use to rate the men we date.''

''Obviously Max—''

''Was off the charts!'' she finished for him. ''Cesar came in a nine. All he lacks is husband skills.'' Taking a risk she said, ''If you're interested in knowing where you weigh in, I'm afraid to tell you.''

''You mean I'm dull and boring like Fred.''

"It's not so much that you're boring as you're morose and very aloof most of the time compared to your
brother for example. You don't know how to play,
and you take your responsibilities so seriously I've
only heard you laugh when you were mocking me."

In an effort not to give away the plot in front of
him, she deliberately gazed at him like he was some
kind of alien species. "In fact you're not like any
other man I know. The normal labels don't apply.
Like I said, robotics pretty well sums you up. You're
the exact opposite of the exciting playboy I planned
to win a proposal from when I came to Europe."

"Tout ce qui brille n'est pas d'or," he muttered.

"I give up. What does that mean?"

One black brow quirked. "All that glitters isn't
gold."

"Spoken like the bona fide cynic you are! If you'll
show me where to go, I'll get started on your packing."

"Follow me."

She fell in line behind him, feasting her eyes on
his sensational male body. He handled the stairs very
well with his cane. His was a powerful physique.
Olivia wouldn't be at all surprised to learn he'd been
a world-class skier before his accident.

According to Cesar, Luc had been in excruciating
pain for several months after getting out of the hospital. She'd listened in horror as he'd told her about
the ghastly accident in Cortina that had almost severed Luc's leg.

No wonder she'd seen deep lines of strain carved
on Luc's handsome features when she'd first been introduced to him aboard the *Piccione*.

This close to him she could tell he'd healed to the

point that the shadows under his eyes and the slightly gaunt look to his cheeks were disappearing. But he hadn't lost the remote quality that put a wall between them. She wanted to tear it down and find out what had caused it in the first place.

When they reached the large master bedroom with its semi-contemporary decor, she thought the shades of blue and burgundy against neutral walls stunning. She lowered her suitcase next to the king-size bed.

Luc sat back against the headboard and rested his leg. "You'll find a valise on the wardrobe shelf. Everything else I'll need should be in that long dresser beneath the window."

She forced her eyes away from the incredible sight he made, then let out a quiet gasp when she looked out the vitrines. It was like getting a bird's-eye view of the whole principality of Monaco. She almost forgot she was supposed to be packing.

The thrill of being here with Luc, of handling his personal clothes, caused her body to tremble, especially with him watching her movements. She soon found everything he would need; a few sport shirts, T-shirts, boxers, cargo pants, cutoffs and a black bathing suit.

"Done." She smiled at him as she closed the lid.

It was a mistake to take another look at him. She might never recover. He resembled some gorgeous virile god lying there on the bed studying her through shuttered eyes.

That's how Greer had first described Max when she'd seen him climb out of the swimming pool at the Splendido Hotel in Portofino. Now Olivia understood why her sister had looked like she'd been shaken to the foundations the night she came back to their hotel room.

Clearing her throat she said, "We'll pack your grooming items in the morning before we leave for the hospital. Anything else I can do for you before I find a room to sleep in?"

Images of crawling on the bed next to him and lying in his arms sent her pulse rate off the charts.

"When we reach the boat, I'll need my leg muscle massaged, but we'll give it a pass for tonight. Do you have an alarm clock?"

She could hardly breathe thinking about touching him and having the right to do it. "I never travel without one."

"Then I'll need to be wakened at six. A limo will be here to take us to the hospital at quarter past the hour."

"I'll be happy to do that."

"If you're hungry, make yourself at home in the kitchen."

"Thank you, but I ate on the plane. Would you like something to eat?"

"I was just finishing my meal when you arrived at the door."

Uh-oh. "Since I interrupted you, I'll go downstairs and clean up."

"That's what I employ a housekeeper for. You're being suspiciously meek and humble all of a sudden."

"It's my true nature coming out."

A burst of mocking laughter escaped his throat. "I have to wonder if you lied to me, and Cesar is on his way over as we speak."

That stung. ''While you wonder all you want, I'm going to pick out a bedroom to sleep in.''

''*Bonne nuit*, Mademoiselle Olivier. If you would be so kind as to turn off the light and shut the door on your way out. Note that I said shut, not slam.''

She could still hear his low evil chuckle after she'd left the room carrying her suitcase. Once she'd peeked in the various bedrooms, each one more elegant and inviting than the last, she chose the room next to Luc's with the same view.

The warm yellow and cream decor delighted her. Substitute the dark furniture for a baby crib and dresser, and it would make a heavenly nursery. All you would have to do is create a connecting door between it and the master bedroom.

Filled with thoughts of what Luc's baby would look like with her as the mother, she got ready for bed in the en suite bathroom.

After setting her travel alarm, she slipped between the sheets of the queen-sized bed, still pinching herself that her plan had worked to the point she was sleeping beneath Luc's roof, next to his own room.

But there was one more thing she had to do, or she wouldn't be able to relax. Turning on her side she picked up the receiver on the nightstand to make a credit card call to Piper. After giving the hotel operator her sister's room number, she waited, then was told Piper had checked out.

While the operator was speaking, Olivia heard a click, like the kind when someone else picks up the phone from another extension.

Luc had his own cell phone to make calls. He was probably spying on her to see if she was trying to reach Cesar. The man in the next room had serious trust issues.

Olivia frowned before thanking the operator and hanging up. Apparently Piper had decided to take a night flight to New York instead of waiting until morning.

Unless Olivia tried to get a number through Greer's new in-laws to reach her in Greece, it looked like she would have to wait until tomorrow for Piper to enlighten her about Luc. While he was in surgery, she would make the call.

Unable to do anything else for the moment, she sank back against the pillows, afraid she would never get to sleep. Luc lay on the other side of the wall. The knowledge that he was awake and might be thinking about her, even if they were negative thoughts, left her breathless.

Visions of him sprawled on top of his mattress were the last images in her mind before her alarm went off seven hours later.

The ground came rushing up to meet the helicopter. Olivia felt slightly unsteady during the rapid descent. This was Luc's normal mode of travel, but it was the first time she'd ridden in one. Way back in Monaco she'd lost her stomach as it took off from the roof of the hospital.

But for most of the flight she forgot to be frightened or sick when her eyes beheld the glorious French and Italian Riviera from the air. People actually lived here, were born here in this paradise!

Olivia couldn't imagine what it would be like to wake up to such beauty every day of her life. To be able to work here, to play, to eat, to go bed and start the whole process all over again the next day in surroundings captured on canvas by the great Impressionists—

Her mind could scarcely comprehend what kind of joy that would bring. But of course Luc would have to be part of that picture, or the magic wouldn't be there no matter how captivating the ambience.

Since she hadn't been able to reach Piper from the hospital, the mystery surrounding Luc loomed larger than ever. Thank goodness Cesar hadn't shown up at the house early to make a liar out of her. Besides, today was not the day for any kind of confrontation.

Though Luc managed to sail through the medical procedure, the doctor had given him a heavy dose of painkiller. She noticed it made him quieter than usual, but other than that he still took charge.

An orderly had helped him from the wheelchair into the helicopter. After they'd landed at the small waterfront area in Vernazza, and he'd been assisted to the ground by the pilot, he was able to walk by leaning on his cane.

Olivia looked all around. The *Piccione*, named for the stylized pigeons on the sails, wasn't in its berth or anywhere else. Puzzled, she turned to Luc. "I don't understand. Where's the catamaran?"

Noise from the rotors of the helicopter must have drowned out her question. After it lifted in the air he moved closer. "What did you say?"

"Why isn't Fabio here to meet us?"

"I forgot to tell you he phoned me while I was in the recovery room. He explained that one of the engines went out, so he had to pull into port at Monterosso. It might take a few days to fix, so he made an arrangement with his friend Giovanni."

Olivia blinked. "What arrangement?"

CHAPTER FOUR

Luc inclined his dark head toward a pathetic-looking sailboat tied up next to the *Piccione*'s berth.

"That dinky thing? You have to be kidding! It looks like something that barely survived the wreck of the *Hesperus*."

He stared at her through veiled eyes. "I've sailed the *Gabbiano* before."

"*Gabbiano?*"

"It means 'seagull.' She's a worthy vessel."

"In other words, we're lucky it floats."

"Fabio tried his best." Luc remained unflappable. "It seems every available boat along this part of the coast has been booked months in advance. I'm afraid it's this or nothing."

His mouth looked taut. Probably the painkiller they'd given him in the hospital was wearing off and he needed to take more. Olivia felt guilty about keeping him standing there, especially when no one was available to help. Worse, the helicopter had disappeared.

"You need to lie down. Come on. We'll get on board while we wait for Giovanni to help us make some other arrangement."

Luc didn't seem to need any urging. It meant his pain level was greater than she'd supposed.

She gathered their bags. Together they walked along the pier. When they reached the boat, she put them down again and told him to use her shoulders for balance. The contact sent little darts of delight through her system.

Slowly he lowered himself into the boat. Even to her uneducated eye it needed an overhaul and paint job inside and out.

In this end of it she saw some fishing gear and one oar, but there were no water skis, no sun mattresses or jet skis—none of the kinds of water sport equipment that came with the luxurious *Piccione.*

She jumped down after Luc, leaving the suitcases on the pier. He held on to her as they descended the steps to the galley below that contained a miniscule kitchen and bathroom with a stall shower. Everything fit together like sardines in a can.

Luc opened the cabin door on the right, with its small window above the dresser and wardrobe. Bunk beds for two took up the rest of the space, leaving little room to maneuver.

Olivia had to confess the place looked clean, yet it was a far cry from the luxury she'd paid for the first time around.

Still, she'd accomplished her first objective. Except for Giovanni, who would probably sleep on one of the padded benches on deck if he couldn't manage to find them something better, she would have Luc to herself for the next ten days.

If it had to be on this sailboat rather than the *Piccione,* she wasn't about to complain. Secretly she was overjoyed to be with him at all.

What she'd give for Piper and Greer to see her now. They hadn't thought she would get this far with him, but they'd underestimated her love for Luc, her determination to win his heart.

The object of her thoughts let go of her and eased

himself onto the bottom bunk. After she helped lift his bandaged leg on top of the spread, he lay back with a deep sigh and closed his eyes.

Quickly she left the cabin and hurried into the kitchen. To her surprise the small fridge was fairly well stocked. She pulled out a bottle of mineral water, then rushed back to him.

The doctor had sent him home with some pills. She drew the bottle from her purse. According to the directions, he could take two every four hours.

"Luc? I've got something for your pain."

His eyelids opened. In the dim light his normal silvery gaze had dimmed to pewter. "Ah...just what the doctor ordered."

Rising up on his elbow he swallowed the pills and drained the bottle. He was thirstier than she realized. It had to be the heat.

"Thank you." He fell back against the pillow and closed his eyes once more.

"When do you think Giovanni will come?"

"I have no idea."

"Could we call him on your cell phone?"

"Of course."

"It's in your trouser pocket."

"No. I gave it to you."

"You did?"

"Hmm. Along with the pills."

"I didn't notice it in my purse." She moved over to the dresser where she'd left it on the top. After rummaging through the contents she turned around. "It's not here."

"Then I have to assume it was left at the hospital by mistake."

Oh, no— Now she couldn't call Piper, either.

"Well—if Giovanni doesn't come soon, I'll walk to a shop near the waterfront and ask to use one of their phones to call him."

"That sounds like a good idea. If you don't mind, I'm going to sleep for a while."

"Good. I need to unpack the suitcases anyway." Oops. She'd left them on the pier.

She retraced her steps to the deck. Thankfully no one had walked off with them. Inside of twenty minutes she'd put everything away. Luc continued to sleep soundly. As Olivia tiptoed around finding places to stash their things, she derived great pleasure watching over him. It was like they were husband and wife.

When she'd arranged everything to her satisfaction, she acquainted herself with the kitchen. There was a tiny cupboard that held some condiments including olive oil. Against the wall was a table and stools you could pull down when you wanted to eat.

A further inspection of the fridge revealed bread, eggs, cheese and ham slices, fruit, wine, soda and some yogurt. Until Giovanni arrived to take over, she could fix Luc the latter. She doubted he would want anything heavier until tomorrow.

As for herself, she was hungry, so she made herself a sandwich and ate it accompanied by a cold orange soda. She loved Italian bread and could make a meal out of it. American bread was squishy and tasteless by comparison.

Once she'd cleaned up her mess, she checked on Luc, who was still out like a light. Helpless to do otherwise, she bent over to look at him.

The arrangement of his strong male features combined with his black hair and olive skin made him a striking man. Unforgettable. She studied him for a long time before tearing herself away to go up on deck and wait for Giovanni.

Most of the boats were out. That was probably the reason why there were so few people walking around. She sat down on one of the benches to take in the view of Vernazza, the same view she'd seen from the cabin window of the *Piccione* over six weeks ago.

Once before she'd marveled at the colorful port village with its cluster of tower-shaped houses, palaces and castles nestled against a backdrop of emerald green steep cliffs. Little had she known then that one Lucien de Falcon would come into her life.

Just knowing he slept below sent a delicious shiver through her body. There was nowhere else in the world she wanted to be. It hurt to realize this was probably the last place he wanted to be, that she was the last woman he wanted to be with. Cesar was the sole reason Luc had been willing to recuperate here instead of his house.

But this was only the first day of their trip. They had nine to go. In that amount of time she intended to make her patient forget all about the brother he'd felt forced to protect from the female he'd branded a groupie.

By the time the boat returned to Vernazza, Luc would be in love with her, no matter what she had to do to make it happen.

A few more minutes of sitting in the hot sun and she felt perspiration break out on her skin beneath her blouse and skirt. Europe was suffering a heat wave right now. She would love to change into her bathing suit and go for a quick swim, but she wanted to wait until Giovanni had come and they'd left the port.

So far no one walking on the pier approached her.

Something had to be holding him up. She decided to check on Luc. If he was awake, she would get the phone number from him and go ashore to make her calls.

As she started for the stairs she heard, *"Signorina— Signorina—"*

Olivia turned in time to see a boy of eleven or twelve waving to her from the pier. She moved closer to him. "Yes?"

"You are waiting for Giovanni?" he asked in heavily accented English.

"Yes!"

"He is not coming."

"How do you know?"

"I know everything!"

"Where is Giovanni?"

"San Remo."

"Is he coming back?"

"No."

"But we need him to sail the boat!"

"His wife. She has a baby!"

A baby— Good heavens.

Her plan to go sailing with Luc had just gone up in smoke!

"Thank you. *Grazie,*" she said to him with a heavy heart.

He smiled. *"Ciao!"*

Devastated by this turn of events, she needed to think up a new plan before Luc found out and had her phone for the helicopter to come and get them. The next thing she knew she'd be deposited at the airport in Nice, left to her own devices.

She could hear Luc now. "Under the circumstances I suggest you go home to New York and make plans with Fabio for another trip. Next summer perhaps? By then Cesar's ardor should have cooled.''

No way was she going to let him dispatch her as if she were so much baggage!

She could go ashore and ask around for someone who knew how to sail and wanted a job on the spot. She would pay them out of her own pocket if she had to. But she didn't have that kind of time. Luc might wake up at any minute.

What to do?

She could hear Greer's voice on their last trip. *What did the Von Trapp Family do when they wanted to get out of Austria and the borders were closed?*

That was it!

Olivia would take the boat out herself. It had a motor. The Mediterranean was smooth as glass right now. She'd run the outboard motor on her dad's rowboat many a time. For that matter she'd driven Fred's boat dozens of times while they'd taken turns waterskiing. How hard could it be?

Later on she would worry about working the sail which was probably in one of the lockers. For now it was imperative she get them away from shore before Luc knew what was happening and sent her packing.

Without wasting another second, she climbed onto the pier and undid the ropes. Once that was accomplished, she got back in the boat and walked to the other end.

She studied the outboard motor and gear shift. It all looked straightforward to her. After seating herself on the bench, she turned the key and pressed the button. The motor revved on cue.

So far so good.

She put the gear in reverse. Luckily there weren't

any boats nearby for her to run into. The boat slowly inched away from the pier. With her hand on the tiller, she made an experimental circle to get the hang of it.

Okay. Here goes.

She pressed on the forward throttle. Off the boat flew. Knowing she should be traveling at a wakeless speed, she decreased the power and headed straight out to sea past the buoys.

Her thoughts flew ahead.

The island of Ischia off of Naples was southeast of Vernazza. All she had to do was head east as far as Lerici where Luc and his cousins had taken them on the *Piccione*. She knew what to look for. After all, it was in those waters she and her sisters had jumped ship in order to get away from the crew. From there she'd head south.

She opened up the throttle. This was a piece of cake.

When she glimpsed other pleasure boats, she gave them wide berth as she navigated through the calm waters. Luc was still asleep. That was good. He needed it.

The motor gave her no trouble. She relaxed and enjoyed the breathtaking view of jewel-like villages dotting the coastline in the far distance.

Olivia decided this was much better than being on the *Piccione*. She had Luc all to herself at last.

A smile curved her lips upward remembering the first time she'd met him. He'd passed himself off as a French chef who cooked for royalty, but to Olivia he'd looked like some sort of dangerous French Adonis.

They'd clashed mightily. Deep down she'd never

been so exhilarated in her life. Now they were clashing again. This time it was a battle to the death, and all the spoils would go to Olivia.

Hunger brought Luc awake. Still disoriented from a drug-induced sleep, he opened his eyes and was surprised to discover it was dark in the cabin.

He checked the time on his watch. Eight-fifteen. He'd been passed out for six hours— Where was Olivia? How come she'd let him sleep this long?

Easing his leg slowly off the bed, he stood up, then had to clutch the upper bunk for a moment. Either he was having serious side effects, or a wind had come up, causing the boat to bob up and down in its berth.

Had Olivia decided Giovanni wasn't coming?

If she'd realized Luc had tricked her, she might have phoned Cesar for help. Luc had no doubts the two of them would have gone off together, leaving him to deal with the situation he'd created.

He felt for his cane resting against the wardrobe and looked out the window expecting to see the lights of Vernazza. To his shock, water surrounded the boat. The *Gabbiano* was at sea!

Who was at the helm?

For one thing, any experienced sailor would have turned on the boat's lights by now. For another, they weren't moving, and there was no sound of the motor.

Leaving the cabin, he used the braille method to make his way to the stairs and ran into a soft, feminine body hurrying down the steps. The impact knocked the cane out of his hand.

"Luc—"

Beneath her surprised cry he detected an underlying note of anxiety. He held on to her in an effort to steady them both. Her heart was pounding so fast he couldn't count the beats. His was thudding, too, but not for the same reason.

During their brief moment of contact, his body became aware of every enticing line and curve molded against him. Her skin still radiated warmth from a hot Mediterranean sun that had gone down some time ago. With his face helplessly buried in her golden curls, he found himself intoxicated by the fresh peach scent emanating from her.

Sensation after sensation bombarded him. Having been in a deep sleep and then suddenly awakened, he felt alive to the primitive side of his male nature. The part of him that recognized this particular female could have been made for him.

If it weren't for the fact that she was a calculating liar and cheat, incapable of being faithful to any man.

He let her go abruptly, then felt for the panel above the stairs to switch on the power and lights.

"So *that's* where they were," she moaned the words. "I looked everywhere but up." She reached for his cane and handed it to him as if that moment in his arms had never happened.

Mon Dieu. Like pure revelation it came to him she'd been playing captain of the *Gabbiano.* Once again he'd underestimated her. This would be the last time...

"Unless there's a reserve tank on board, we're out of gas. That's what I was coming down to tell you."

Her voice sounded steady enough now, but he hadn't imagined her nervousness seconds earlier. He would never forget the way she'd clung to him for that infinitesimal moment when the darkness had stripped away her bravado.

He found himself drawn to the alluring design of her mouth whose shape reminded him of a half-opened rose. Something told him that if he were ever fool enough to taste it, then it meant he hadn't learned life's most important lesson.

"When did you decide to take matters into your own hands?"

"This afternoon a young boy ran along the pier and informed me Giovanni wasn't coming."

Luc had to give her credit for not pretending that she didn't know what he was talking about.

"Why couldn't he make it?"

She folded her arms. "Suppose you tell me? If I didn't know better, I would think you'd set me up so I'd go back to New York and forget about my Riviera trip. You would love to see the last of me. Admit it!"

"I admit it would be better for my brother who's too blindsided by you and his latest win to see through to the real Mademoiselle Duchess."

Her eyes narrowed. "The *real* me?"

"That's right. A heartless, materialistic, ambitious vixen who does whatever comes naturally to her without any compunction. I could tell you more about yourself, but first I need to switch tanks. In the meantime you can bring me a hot dinner while I find us a cove to spend the night."

Vixen my foot!

Olivia banged things around in the tiny kitchen. Heartless? Materialistic? Ambitious?

A seer wasn't required for Olivia to figure out what kind of women had thrown themselves at him over the years. She supposed being born a Falcon had made him and Cesar natural targets for the type of avaricious female he'd accused her of being. It had turned Luc mean and hurtful, and so suspicious of the opposite sex his natural feelings were buried.

That's why her sisters had tried so hard to dissuade her from chasing after him. She could understand why. He was a thirty-three-year-old misogynist more hardened than Max before Greer came into his life.

But not all women were opportunistic. Far from it. Whether a prince or a pauper, the majority wanted to find a great and lasting love and remain true to that one man.

Somehow she would show Luc she was the latter.

Instead of retaliating because of his cruel attack, she would ignore every barb and salvo intended to destroy her. When he realized she could take whatever he dished out, and that she wasn't about to go away, he would be forced to see that her heart was pure. In time she would wear him down with her love until he had no choice but to love her back.

Tonight he wanted a hot meal. She would get busy and give him the most scrumptious dinner she could prepare with the ingredients at hand. Now that he'd turned on the power, she could make him an omelet à la Olivia, and homemade bruschetta with the olive oil she'd seen in the cupboard.

If he could play a French chef, so could she. Turnabout was fair play. She bet he thought she couldn't cook worth a darn, especially not under these circumstances. Well he could think again.

While she was preparing cappuccino, she heard the engine rev. Soon she felt the boat moving through the water once more. Thankful he'd sailed this boat before and knew where and how to navigate in the darkness, she got his plate ready and carried everything up on deck.

He sat on the bench with the tiller in one hand, his long powerful legs extended in front of him. She noted he was still dressed in chinos and the tan sport shirt he'd worn to the hospital.

The collar flapped against his firm jawline where she could see the shadow of his dark beard. Combined with his black hair disheveled by the sea breeze, his potent sexuality turned her insides to liquid.

"Here you go." She put everything on the bench next to him. His gaze darted to the food she'd fixed as if he couldn't believe his eyes. When he finally looked up at her, she turned away and said she'd be right back. Olivia didn't dare gloat in front of him.

In a minute she'd rejoined him with her food and took a sip of the steaming brew. It tasted even better than she'd thought. Putting in extra sugar gave it that extra punch they could use.

To her satisfaction she saw that he'd already swallowed half his food. Most of his coffee was gone, too.

"More bruschetta?" She piled another couple of rounds on his plate while he finished munching the last of his.

He flicked her penetrating glance. "How did you learn to make it?" Upon asking the question, he devoured the ones she'd given him.

"Greer found out Max loves it, so she practiced fixing it at home. Piper and I helped." She had to bite her lip to keep from asking him if he liked it.

Once he'd drained the last of his coffee, he put everything aside. She expected to see some softening of his features after the feast she'd just prepared for his royal highness. Instead they'd gone all chiseled looking. His eyes pierced hers. "Do you have any idea where we are?"

"Sort of. I was headed for Ischia."

"You mean you just took off and hoped for the best."

"Well...yes. I mean, how hard is it? The sun sets in the west, so I went east and kept the coastline in view."

He rubbed his eyes with his palms. She half wondered if he hadn't wanted to shake her unconscious, and didn't know what else to do with them. Taking out the sailboat without his knowledge had been a foolhardy, if not dangerous thing to do, and she knew it. But she'd been desperate.

"Relax, Luc. We're alive, safe and well fed." If he wasn't going to compliment her on her culinary skills, then she would.

He lifted his head with a grimace. "You took advantage of a calm sea and ran the boat at full throttle. It drained the first tank of gas. The other one is only a reserve tank and doesn't hold nearly as much. We'll be damn lucky if we make it to Monte Cristo."

Her eyes opened wide. "You're kidding! I've always wanted to go there." She smiled. "I didn't realize I'd brought the boat this far!"

"As I said earlier, life is just one big game to you, but in this case it could have cost lives if another boat hadn't seen us in the fading light. When you're on the water, the ability to judge distances is hampered and can present serious problems."

She ate the last of her omelet before responding. "I came down to get you as soon as I realized we might be hard to spot. Don't worry. I wouldn't have let anything happen to you in your condition. If we'd run out of gas, I would have figured out how to put up the sail.''

"There *is* no sail.''

No sail?

"But I thought that locker container—''

"You should have looked before you took our lives into your own inexperienced hands.''

It was the story of her life, and a reminder of her impulsive trip to Monza with Cesar. But Luc didn't have any room to talk. "If I leaped, it's because you led me to believe this sailboat was a worthy vessel. Your exact words!

"If you already knew there wasn't a sail, it means you never planned for this trip to come off in the first place, so it's your fault if we're stuck out here.''

He didn't bother to deny her accusation. To her chagrin he stared at her like she was a child having a temper tantrum. "You may end up having to row us to safety. In fact you'll have to slip overboard and tow us to shore should we be fortunate enough to reach the island before we're running on fumes.''

His gaze produced a breathless sensation inside her as it wandered the length of her body still clad in the skirt and blouse she'd worn to the hospital. "I suggest you put on something more practical for the ordeal ahead.''

Olivia's first instinct was to engage him in another verbal skirmish, but that's what he wanted. To make her so mad she'd go away forever at the first opportunity.

She rose to her feet, gathering their plates and mugs. "How's your pain? Can I bring you another pill?''

"I'm fine right now.''

Even if he wasn't, he wouldn't admit to it. The medication had made him sleep so soundly, he'd been unaware of what she'd done until it was too late. Naturally he didn't plan on taking any more risks with her around.

"How about another cappuccino?"

"Later."

"That's probably a better idea. I'll be able to give your leg muscles a massage at the same time," she said before disappearing below with a secret grin.

Once she'd cleaned up the kitchen, she entered the cabin and changed into her emerald green bathing suit. It was the most modest two-piece she'd been able to find in Kingston, but that wasn't saying much.

On impulse she drew a navy T-shirt out of Luc's drawer and pulled it on over her suit. It fell to mid-thigh and made her feel less exposed. After removing her sandals, she put on her sneakers.

According to Greer who'd done the research, Monte Cristo was a rocky, uninhabited island. If she had to jump off the boat, she needed something to protect her feet.

On the way up the stairs she heard the engine start to act up. It kind of sputtered, ran, then sputtered again before stopping altogether. She swallowed hard. They were out of gas.

The idea of rowing didn't appeal, but they had no choice now. She walked over to one of the benches and lifted the top.

"What are you doing?" he asked grimly.

"I was hoping I might find some gloves in one of these lockers. I used to do a lot of rowing with Daddy on the river and can already feel the blisters forming."

"You must live under a lucky star because the island's about forty yards straight ahead. Here!" He threw her a life jacket from the bench locker where he'd been sitting. "Put it on, then grab the rope at the front end of the boat and jump in the water.

"You'll feel the bottom at about twenty yards. It shouldn't be difficult to pull the boat after you and find a place to secure the rope."

She supposed she deserved his cavalier treatment of her. Besides, he knew she was a strong swimmer. He'd seen her dive off the *Piccione* to swim twenty times that distance in order to reach the port of Lerici.

"What about sharks?"

He cocked his head. "I don't recall you worrying about them before."

"You told me there'd been a sighting of a great white near the Marche/Abruzzo border when we were on the *Piccione*. It wasn't until later I found out it wasn't a lie."

"I'm glad you remembered our little chat. Be sure to slip into the water quietly. If I should see one, I'll tell you to let go of the rope and swim like the devil for shore."

"That's very reassuring."

It was a warm night, even with the breeze blowing from the northwest. If there was a moon, she couldn't see it in the mist that seemed to hover around them. In fact she could barely distinguish between the water and the outline of land exposed like the back of a turtle.

"Tell me when you're ready and I'll light a flare to help you see."

She reached for the end of the rope and made her way to the edge of the boat. "I'm waiting—"

There was a hissing sound before light illuminated his handsome features and the water surrounding the boat. It was a surreal sight.

She climbed up on the side and jumped, pleasantly surprised to discover the water wasn't as cold as she'd feared. Once she'd surfaced, she struck out for the island doing the side stroke. It enabled her to tug the boat along behind her without getting tangled in it. At first she had to pull hard, but little by little she made progress.

Luc must have known these waters well to have gauged how soon she'd be able to touch the sea floor with her sneakers. Though she would never admit it to him, once she walked on dry land, she was glad she hadn't met with anything out there in search of prey.

Quickly while the flare lasted, she found a good-sized rock and tied the rope the best she could. Then she shouted to Luc to toss the other rope end in the water. Within a few minutes, she'd pulled the boat around to secure it to another rock. Hopefully she'd done a good enough job that the boat wouldn't float away from the shore during the night.

At least here they would be protected from the many cruise ships and large ocean-going yachts and tankers passing back and forth in the night.

By the time she'd swum to the boat, the flare had burned out. Luc lowered the ladder over the side for her. She grabbed hold of it and swung herself up. He surprised her by gripping her waist to ease her to the deck.

"You shouldn't have done that!" she cried in a shaky voice. His touch had sent what felt like an electric current running through her body. "Your leg!"

As he slowly removed his hands, they seemed to trail over her hips before letting her go. "No harm was done. I put all the weight on my good one."

"Nevertheless you shouldn't have had so much activity this soon after leaving the hospital. Let's get you off your feet and back to bed." She handed him his cane and followed him below.

He nodded toward the bathroom. "You use the shower first." There was an underlying tone of authority in his suggestion that tolerated no argument.

"I'll get my things."

When she went to move past him, the confines of the passageway were so tight, her body brushed against the hardness of his. Her breath caught to feel his flesh and blood warmth. She didn't let it out until she reached the cabin and rummaged in the drawer for a pair of shorts and a white T-shirt she would wear to bed.

On her way back out, Luc had cleared the doorway leaving space between them. She moaned inwardly, wishing he were still in the way so she could experience the thrill of the contact of their bodies again, no matter how brief.

Once she reached the bathroom and closed the door, she clung to the sink for something to hold on to until her trembling stopped.

Earlier in the day she'd put their toiletries in the cabinet. After a few minutes of attempting to get herself under some semblance of control, she took a shower and washed the seawater out of her hair.

Several towels were folded above the cabinet. She pulled one down and wrapped it around her wet curls. Then she rinsed out her swimsuit and Luc's T-shirt before leaving them over the towel rack to dry.

The last thing she did was brush her teeth before going to the kitchen to fix Luc another cappuccino. When she entered the bedroom, she discovered he'd changed out of his clothes and was half-lying on the bottom bunk wearing one of the pairs of cutoffs she'd packed for him.

"Here you go."

He took the mug from her. "You're not having any?"

"Too much caffeine makes me restless this time of night." She got down on her haunches. It put their eyes at the same level. His gleamed like sterling silver in the cabin light. "Where shall I begin your massage? How does it have to be done? I don't want to hurt you."

Before answering her, he drank his coffee, then set the mug on the floor. "I think I'll forego the experience tonight."

She eyed him anxiously. "Because you're in too much pain?"

He seemed to hesitate, as if choosing his words carefully. "Because you've done enough for one night."

Olivia sucked in her breath. "What you really mean is, I put our lives in danger today and you wish me thousands of miles away from here."

His head went back against the pillow, but his eyes remained trained on her. "Since it's a moot point, what I wish doesn't matter."

Luc was covering up for his discomfiture. "You're hurting, aren't you," she persisted.

"No. It's only a mild irritation." He sounded as if he meant it, but she would never know for sure. "The doctor drew fluid out of my knee in several places. It relieved pressure that's been building, *Dieu merci.*''

She inspected the visible signs of the operation done on him months earlier, then raised her eyes to his once more. ''Cesar said you almost lost your leg. Thank God you didn't!''

''I was very fortunate.'' He put one arm behind his head. ''The doctors were able to reattach the severed nerves, restoring circulation. Exercise and massages did the rest.''

''Are you sure I can't rub your leg down?''

''Tomorrow will be soon enough.''

Olivia shook her head. ''What a ghastly ordeal that must have been for you.''

''It was worse for Nic.''

She shuddered. ''Cesar told me about his fiancée. I can't imagine losing someone I loved, let alone in such a horrible accident.''

Luc didn't respond to that, but she felt his emotional withdrawal. ''I'd rather not talk about it.''

''Of course not. I'm sorry. Is there anything else I can do for you before I go to bed?''

''Shut off the light.''

CHAPTER FIVE

FOR a few moments there they'd actually been conversing without her feeling Luc's animosity. But as soon as Olivia had brought Cesar into the conversation, a barrier slid into place like one of those cloaking devices in a science fiction movie.

It hurt to be shut out so totally. As she started to get up, her towel unraveled, revealing a head of damp, unruly curls before it fell to the floor. When she reached for it, she heard him whisper something unintelligible.

"You *are* in pain."

"Give it a rest, Olivia."

He'd delivered his last comment with an edge intended to warn her off. She wouldn't be learning anything more from him tonight. Defeated for the time being, she retraced her steps to the bathroom and hung up her towel.

On the way back to the cabin, she made a detour to the kitchen for more mineral water and his pills. "I'll put these on the floor by your bed in case you need them."

Without expecting a response, she shut off the cabin light. There was a ladder at the end of the beds. She climbed it to the top bunk and eased herself beneath the covers.

"Luc?"

When she heard the expletive that came out of him, she winced.

"Doesn't that wild Duchess brain of yours ever shut down for one second?"

"It can't when I know we're out of gas."

"Someone will come by eventually."

"To this deserted place? What if we run out of food first?"

"You saw Giovanni's fishing gear. You can catch us our meals. If that doesn't appeal, you could always swim to Elba for help."

Olivia blinked. "How far away is it?"

"It might take you an hour."

An hour—

"If it's too much of a challenge—"

"I'll do it if I have to, but first I think we should try to flag down a passing boat. I know—we'll set off another flare to get their attention."

"I'm afraid I used the only one left to help you see what you were doing."

"I already knew what I was doing! You should have saved it for an emergency," she grumbled.

A taunting laugh escaped his throat. "*That* from the woman who stole out of Vernazza without a map, compass, or a clue as to what you were doing."

"I got us this far didn't I?"

"You don't really want me to answer that question, do you?"

She turned on her other side and pounded her pillow.

"Look on the bright side, *mademoiselle*. Tomorrow you can hunt for buried treasure. Your Riviera trip doesn't have to be a complete loss."

"The Count of Monte Cristo already found it." She fumed. "Besides, I saw the movie, and it was filmed in the Maltese Islands."

"I've been there on the *Piccione*."

She lifted her head, alert because he'd offered something without her having to pry it out of him. "When?"

"Several years ago."

Olivia tried to sit up all the way, but her head bumped the ceiling of the cabin. She lay back down again. "You and Fabio must go back a long way."

"The *Piccione* was Max's boat before he gave it to Fabio."

Gave it— She bumped her head again. "He must have had a good reason to part with anything so fabulous."

"The best of reasons. Fabio and his whole family fished for a living. His parents, their fishing boat, everything was lost at sea during a violent storm. Max was close friends with him growing up. Knowing he had a pregnant wife and two brothers to support, he let him have the boat to establish a charter business."

Olivia's throat closed up with raw emotion. Did Greer know that piece of information about her remarkable husband?

"By your silence, I realize that kind of generosity is anathema to you. It may surprise you even more to learn that Fabio has paid Max back every lire for it through hard work."

Luc's stinging barbs found their mark, but she'd promised herself she wouldn't rise to the bait.

"Thank you for confiding in me. Before you gave me this insight into Max, I loved him because my sister loved him. But now, I love my new brother-in-law for my own reasons. You've given me a priceless gift. It has been worth taking all the abuse you've heaped my way."

"Material things matter much more to you than I thought. Work it right, and you'll be able to benefit from Max's generosity for years to come, Cesar or no Cesar."

It was such a heartless comment, she groaned into her pillow.

There had to be a way to reach Luc. He wasn't born believing the worst about people. That world-weary derisiveness he wore like a shroud was the result of one terrible act against him.

Piper had been told what it was, but there was no way to reach her without a phone.

Greer knew the truth, yet until she returned from her honeymoon and could enlighten Olivia, the status quo would continue to prevail with Luc who was well ensconced in his invisible fortress, withdrawn and utterly impervious.

She flipped over on her back, wide awake. Her immediate problem was to figure out how they were going to get off this island anytime soon. If no one came by to help them tomorrow, they could always start out the next day by rowing.

It would be hard going with only one oar, but they might not have any other choice. Unless she could find something on the island she could use for another paddle...

As she took mental stock of their provisions, she realized they only had enough food for a couple of days, if they were careful. Part of the excitement of a trip like this was to go ashore each day at a different heavenly spot. She'd planned to buy various items in the local markets of the ports and bring them back to the boat to cook and eat.

In the event that it might be several days before

they could get more gas and food, she would act on Luc's suggestion and fish for their breakfast in the morning.

She was no novice to the sport. Her dad had been an expert fly fisherman. He'd taught a lot of tricks to his daughters, his precious pigeons as he'd loved to call them.

Along with their mom they'd done a lot of outdoor activities at one of his favorite lakes in the Adirondacks. Tomorrow she would get up with the sun and find out just how good a pupil she'd been.

Relieved to have a plan, any plan, Olivia rolled over on her stomach praying sleep would come so she wouldn't be tempted to climb down the ladder and seek comfort from Luc. In the mood he was in, she could easily imagine him strangling her with his bare hands.

Hands that had grasped her waist and hips earlier tonight to haul her into the boat. Hands she could have sworn had lingered for an overly long moment against her wet skin. She still felt feverish from their warmth.

"Knock, knock. Ready or not, I've brought you breakfast in bed."

Luc had been in that hazy place where one hovered between waking and sleeping. When he opened his eyes, he discovered the sun was already well up in the sky. Olivia walked toward him with a mug in one hand, a plate of food in the other. Even out of the sun, her curls gleamed like spun gold.

"On a scale of one to ten, ten being highest, what's your pain level this morning?" Her cheery disposition irritated the hell out of him.

"Minus one."

"If that's true, then why the scowl on your face? Don't you know it takes more muscles to frown than smile?"

Ciel! On a scale of one to ten, ten being the highest for the most exasperating, impossible female he'd ever known, she rated a twenty!

That tantalizing body of hers was dressed in the same shorts and shirt she'd worn to bed last night. Among their many gifts, the Duchess triplets were blessed with long shapely legs. No one was more aware of that fact than Luc as she approached looking wide-awake, and for want of a better word…exhilarated.

"It's another gorgeous day." She put his coffee on the floor next to him. "I've been up for hours watching for a passing boat to wave down, but so far no luck."

He eased his back against the wall so he could take the plate from her. The mouthwatering aroma of grilled fish hot off the skillet wafted past his nostrils. His eyes took in the expert presentation of toast points and orange slices arranged as if he'd just been served the pièce de résistance at a five-star restaurant.

One bite of the delicious, light flaky meat expertly filleted, seasoned and sauteed in olive oil, and he shot her a questioning glance. "This is fresh sea bass!"

"That's right. I caught it a little while ago. There was a school of juvenile fish playing around the rocks. We don't have to worry about starving to death before we're rescued."

If he didn't know for a fact there was no freezer on board to keep fish on ice, he wouldn't have believed her. She'd actually found food for them and could prepare it like a master chef?

"There are four more fillets in the pan, so if you want refills just holler. I'll be in the kitchen cleaning up." She took away the mineral water bottle he'd drained during the night.

With the combined flavor of the oranges, fish had never tasted so good to him before. Even the coffee was different. She'd added cocoa. He devoured everything between mouthfuls of the steaming brew, stunned by her resourcefulness and a lot of other things he wasn't disposed to examine right now.

A few minutes later she reappeared in the doorway. "More?"

"No. I'll eat the rest for lunch."

"Whatever you say. When I come back, I'll give you that massage."

His muscles had tightened up on him during the night. A massage would feel good. He removed the covers and turned over on his stomach so his injured leg would be closest to her.

Soon he felt her presence as she knelt at the side of the bunk. The subtle flowery fragrance from the soap she used in the shower drifted in his direction, intoxicating him.

"Okay. I'm ready for your instructions."

"Start with my foot and knead your way up my calf, but no farther."

"All right." She molded her hand to his heel and began to caress the pad with gentle insistence. Her nimble fingers seemed to know instinctively where to rub using the right pressure. With slow deliberation, she worked her magic from his toes to his calf.

He didn't have to tell her to use the flat of her palm

to wiggle the fleshy part, thereby loosening those muscles. Her touch was instinctive. He could feel its healing effect as his whole body began to relax.

"How am I doing?"

Luc was afraid to tell her. He didn't dare admit it to himself. "If you did this service for Cesar before the race, then I can understand why he would want you around."

"I'll take that as a compliment," she said without missing a breath. Her glib response frustrated him no end. "Would you like your neck and shoulders massaged, too?"

She'd probably done all this and more for his brother. Luc sucked in his breath. "Just keep up what you're doing for a minute longer, and I won't require another session until bedtime."

"What about your water therapy?"

"I'll go for a brief swim later in the day after my lunch has digested."

"We'll both swim. In the meantime, you can read the latest thriller I brought with me while I go hunting for treasure."

He lifted his head. "Owing to the fact that the fabulous fortune buried in the grotto of Monte Cristo didn't exist outside Dumas's imagination, I thought you'd given up on the idea."

"Wasn't it you who told me 'all that glitters isn't gold'?" Her hand gave him a final pat. "There may be treasure lurking here not instantly recognizable to the naked eye."

To his chagrin she stood up, thereby ending these few moments of sheer physical pleasure. "I understand from Greer the island only takes up six square miles. I probably won't be gone exploring for more than a couple of hours. While I'm away, you can shower and read at your leisure. I've left the book on the dresser.''

Olivia Duchess never did anything without an agenda. What was she up to now? ''Good luck spouse hunting,'' he muttered as she started to leave the cabin.

She paused in the doorway. ''Thanks. Maybe I'll run into a heartthrob who's scuba diving off his yacht.''

After she disappeared, he eased himself out of bed with the help of his cane and walked over to the window to survey the situation.

In a minute he saw her splashing through the water to the shore. She took the time to inspect the ropes still tied by the rocks before she began her jog around the desolate island.

It didn't matter that the surface resembled the moonscape. At this point Luc was beginning to realize this woman was a self-starter who made her own luck. Nothing kept her down. No hill was too hard for her to climb.

Her resilience under stress was almost as astounding as her fearless predilection for attempting the impossible and getting away with it. Only the Duchess sisters could have made their escape out the second-story window of his parents' villa in the middle of the night without making a sound or injuring themselves.

He might even have admired her daring if he hadn't known she'd risked life and limb to watch Cesar race in the Grand Prix a few hours later.

Luc's brother had been so flattered to learn that he was the sole reason she'd come to Monaco—that she'd tossed her American lover aside for him—it was no wonder he couldn't see through her master plan which had been to become Madame Cesar de Falcon.

It was a stroke of genius on her part to run away from him after his win at Monza, pretending she really wasn't interested in him after all.

Knowing how many other women had tried and failed to get his ring on their finger, she'd done the one thing guaranteed to bring him to his knees.

Beautiful, amoral Olivia Duchess was the perfect match for Luc's dashing, amoral brother.

Little did Cesar know that while she was waiting for him to catch up to her, she'd made for Ischia last night while Luc had been asleep, hoping to catch a prince. There was no limit to her ambition, as Cesar would find out one of these days. Luc wished them the joy of each other.

But in the meantime they were stuck on Monte Cristo, and she was unable to be a temptation to anyone since no one in the world knew where she was except Luc.

While they were marooned here, it might be an interesting experiment to see how long she could keep up this adventurous facade before she started to crack. Every human had a breaking point. More than anyone else, Luc would appreciate learning what it was. Even better, he'd enjoy watching it happen.

Curious to know if Cesar was hot on the trail yet, he walked back to the bunk and reached inside the pillowcase for his cell phone. He wasn't surprised to see a list of callers that included everyone close to him except his brother.

Taking advantage of Olivia's absence, he phoned Nic, who'd left half a dozen messages.

"Luc—it's a relief to hear your voice. How's the leg?"

"Couldn't be better. What's the real reason behind all your calls?"

"Max phoned to find out if I knew where Olivia is. I thought she was in Monza with Cesar, but apparently he said she left after the race and went to see you. Later I found out that Greer spoke to her at your house night before last. What's going on?"

Good question.

Night before last Luc had listened in while Olivia had tried to reach Piper in Genoa. That meant the first phone call to the house had been from Greer, not Cesar. Why had Olivia pretended otherwise?

"Greer and Piper are both upset because they've had no contact with Olivia since," Nic explained further. "If you know where she is, tell her to do everyone a favor and get in touch with her sisters so they'll stop worrying. Max would like to enjoy his honeymoon."

Luc chewed on his lower lip for a moment. "Right now she's playing a very dangerous game."

"What do you mean?"

He glanced out the window once more. There was no sign of Olivia yet. "How much time have you got?"

"It's been a half hour since we ate lunch. Time for your water therapy."

After finishing off the fish, Luc had sat in the sun to read, effectively shutting Olivia out. Since she'd returned from her exploration of the island, something

about him had been different. She couldn't put her
finger on it, but he was less approachable, which
didn't come as any great surprise. He'd removed the
elastic wrap and bandages where the doctor had
drawn off the fluid. Olivia couldn't tell the procedure
had even been done.

But maybe his leg was hurting him, and he didn't
want her to know.

If that was the case, hopefully a swim might make
it feel better. He'd donned his black suit in anticipa-
tion. The trick was to get him in and out of the boat
without injury.

Olivia stood up from the padded bench and removed the T-shirt she'd been wearing over her swimsuit to protect her shoulders. Because the sun was so
strong, Luc had also put on a shirt he'd left unbut-
toned.

She walked over to him and took the book from
his hands. By the way his features seemed to harden
as his narrowed gaze swept up her body to confront
hers, it had been the wrong thing to do. But it was
too late to worry about that now.

"Ready?"

He rose to his full height and started to remove his
shirt. She put the book on the bench so she could help
him. He had an extraordinary male physique. The desire to touch him had become a driving need, but he
shrugged out of his shirt so fast, she was denied the
pleasure of physical contact.

Before she could catch her breath, he dove off the
side of the boat into the water which was at a depth
of about twelve feet. She followed him in and swam
circles around him while he tread water.

The sun had warmed his olive skin, bringing color

to the surface. His eyes glinted silver. With his wet black hair sleeked back, and drops of water beading his dark brows and eyelashes, he was the personification of male beauty. As she looked at him an ache passed through Olivia's body so intense, she looked away.

When she felt she was under control again, she swam over to him. "If you'll lie back and let me support your head and shoulders, you'll be able to exercise your leg the way you need to."

"Since when did you become a physical therapist?"

Olivia forced herself not to react to his rancor. "In the early stages of cancer, mother enjoyed a swim if we girls helped her. She tired easily."

In the silence that followed her remark, she could feel him digesting what she'd said. Then without her having to say anything else, he turned over on his back as a signal she should help him.

Hoping he couldn't tell she was trembling, she slid her hands under his arms and steadied him while he propelled them around with his legs. Cocooned as he was in her arms, she could bury her face in his hair and he was none the wiser that she was in a state of ecstasy.

"Was skiing your favorite sport?" she asked, trying to keep her voice steady.

"One of them."

"How soon does the doctor say you can ski again?"

"Never again." There was a wealth of emotion in those words.

"Knowing you, you'll probably end up an Olympic swimmer."

Before she could blink, he'd jerked out of her arms and had turned so he was treading water in front of her. "You don't know anything about me."

"I know *of* you," she fought against the bitterness in his accusation. "Despite the fact that you almost lost your leg in that accident, Cesar told me how you gave CPR to several of the injured skiers and kept them alive until the paramedics arrived. Your action saved their lives. That kind of heroism is rare."

His eyes clouded with emotion she couldn't decipher. "It couldn't save Nina's."

"According to Cesar, no one could have done anything for Nic's fiancée. Your little brother lives in awe of you, you know."

She thought his face lost color. "Then we're not talking about the same person."

The next thing she knew, Luc had rolled over on his stomach. Like a torpedo, he took off for deeper water, leaving Olivia to ponder his words.

She felt the weight of them as she headed for the boat and pulled herself up the rungs of the ladder. Joy had gone out of her day because she realized that something terrible had torn the two brothers apart.

If Luc had serious issues with Cesar, then it explained why Cesar was so intimidated by his elder brother despite his hero worship of him. And somewhere in the middle of all this sat Olivia.

It killed her that two wonderful, remarkable brothers had reached such a terrible impasse in their lives. Though her sisters irritated her at times, Olivia couldn't comprehend being estranged from them. Life wouldn't be worth living if that were the case. No wonder Luc and his brother were both suffering.

She could see him in the distance. It didn't look as

if he would be coming back for a while. Since she couldn't bear to sit around on the boat in agony because of all the things she didn't know about the Falcon brothers' complicated relationship, she decided to get started on her latest project.

Once she'd pulled on Luc's navy T-shirt and had found her sneakers, she grabbed another of her own T-shirts and went ashore to hunt for rocks. There were all kinds with interesting pink and red colors the size of Ping-Pong balls strewn across the island.

It took her a couple of hours to gather them into a sizable pile. She carried them in the T-shirt she'd made into a pouch, and took it down to the water's edge to wash them off.

If they were polished, they'd be quite pretty.

Pleased with the results, she lugged them back to the boat. To her surprise, the sun had dropped a lot lower in the sky. She'd been out longer than she'd realized.

When Luc saw her on the ladder, he put the book aside and took the pouch from her while she climbed into the boat.

He lifted it up and down, as if trying to guess its weight. That mocking smile was in evidence once more. "What have we got here?"

"Treasure. Want to take a peek?" She plucked the pouch from his hand and put it on the bench to open it.

He stared at the contents. "I don't see anything but a pile of rocks."

"Your psyche's too scarred to see their individual beauty."

She felt his body stiffen and rejoiced that she'd hit

a nerve. It was about time she won one round in the battle for his love.

"For your information, I'm going to start a new business with these."

"What happened to your calendar business?"

"It was Greer's idea, and Piper's the artist. I've decided I want to do something solely on my own for a change."

"These stones are too big to make into pendants."

She let that intentional dig go by. "Not pendants. Paperweights. The perfect gift for the discerning customer."

A deep chuckle rolled out of Luc.

"Laugh now, but one day I'll be laughing all the way to the bank."

"You're hoping to make a fortune on these?" he taunted.

"I *know* I will."

"Why bother when the Prince of Monaco will be able to shower you with everything you could ever want."

Good. Luc hadn't forgotten. He possessed a mind that worked like a steel trap.

"I'd rather marry for love, and earn my own money. There's tons to be made on the Internet. My sisters and I found that out when we advertised our calendars online."

His hands went to his hips in a totally masculine gesture. "Just how are you going to get people to buy your rocks?"

"If you had any romance in your soul, you wouldn't have to ask that question."

"Romance…" He made it sound like an evil word.

"Yes. There's probably no more famous adventure novel in the whole world than the Count of Monte Cristo. Even if people haven't read the book, they've heard of it.

"My hook will read, 'Enjoy a piece of living history. Treasure straight from the Island of Monte Cristo. Every paperweight is different in size, shape and color. Beneath its polished surface lives the story of two men: Abbe Faria who loved God, Edmond Dantes who loved revenge more.'"

Luc was so quiet at this point she said, "I'm thinking of charging fifty dollars a piece. It's not too steep for the person looking for that perfect gift for the discerning shopper.

"In a way I hope we're not rescued for another day because I need to gather as many rocks as I can. After we leave here, I'd like to head to Elba and collect rocks from there. In case my business takes off, I could sell them as mementos of Napoleon's exile. History buffs would love them!"

"I thought you were anxious to get to Ischia."

"I am, but a few more days delay shouldn't matter."

"What if the Prince is gone when we arrive?"

"Then I'll use you and your connections to find out where he went." She smiled and stretched. "This trip is turning out a lot better than I'd hoped. In a way I'm glad Fabio's boat wasn't available. If we'd gone with him, we wouldn't have come here, and I wouldn't have stumbled onto my future."

He frowned. "Aren't you getting ahead of yourself? These rocks might turn out to be a weight around your neck."

"No." She shook her head. "I can feel success in my bones. It has made me hungry. What do you want for dinner?"

"Surprise me."

"Would you like it served on deck, or below?"

"Below."

"I don't blame you. To think the Mediterranean is known for its unmatched beauty, and here we are marooned on the only ugly, flat rock pile out in the middle of nowhere."

His lips twitched. He was gorgeous when he even halfway smiled.

Relieved that the dark mood he'd been in earlier seemed to have passed, she headed for the galley determined that one day soon she would break him down enough to learn his secrets.

Half an hour later she told him dinner was ready. They ate a meal of ham and cheese melts at the little drop-down table. She found a bottle of wine, and threw in some plums for dessert.

"Tell me about these robots of yours," she said after biting into the fruit. "If we brought one out here, could it pick up rocks for me?"

He drank some more wine. "The one I'm working on is an automobile that can drive itself and enter a war zone to deliver supplies in hostile territory. If you want a worker robot, the Japanese have developed ones that pick fruit, scour sewers, clean the windows of skyscrapers. The list is endless."

Totally fascinated, she leaned closer to him. "I want to hear more about your invention. How long have you been working on it?"

"While I was at the University of Parma a few

years ago, I designed a prototype of an intelligent vehicle. The hardware and software platform enabled it to drive automatically in real traffic conditions.''

''How far did your car end up traveling without a driver?''

''Two thousand miles of Italian motorways and back roads.''

''No accidents?''

''None.''

She shook her head. ''How incredible! I would love to have seen it. Like a remote-control car without the remote.''

''That's a good way to put it. Inside it's interfaced with many layers of sensors, cameras and computers that react on multiple levels.''

''Something like the human brain?''

''Close.''

''What made you go into that aspect of engineering?''

''I grew up reading science fiction, and imagined myself creating a world of robots to do my bidding.''

''Since Cesar dreamed of being at the wheel to drive fast cars himself, he obviously didn't share your interest.''

The comment had just slipped out because the joy of interacting with Luc had made her forget how much he despised her. But the mere mention of Cesar and the tension was back. She could tell by the way his hard-muscled body stiffened.

''Why is it that whenever his name is brought into the conversation, you act as if I'd committed high treason?''

When he refused to answer her, something snapped

inside her. "Would you rather we talked about the reason why you're so certain he doesn't worship the ground you walk on?"

CHAPTER SIX

LUC'S eyes pierced hers like lasers. "Have you always gone where angels feared to tread?"

"My sisters would tell you yes."

"If you're that curious, why don't you discuss it with Cesar the next time you see him."

"You mean I have your permission?"

"Would it stop you if I said no?"

She let his question hang in the air and got up to clear the table. "Tell me something. Are you just naturally bitter because it's a trait inherited through your Falcon genes? Or was it the tragedy that turned you into a dark facsimile of your former self?"

He bit out something unintelligible while she washed the dishes and straightened up the kitchen. When she reached the doorway, she paused. "Do you need another massage before we turn in?"

"I've exercised it enough for one day."

You have your answer, Olivia. "I'll go up on deck and get the book."

"I finished it."

Her eyes closed tightly for a minute. "Good. Now I'll have something to read before I go to sleep. Anything else you need from above?"

"No."

Olivia had thought she could withstand whatever verbal blows he thrust at her, no matter how mean or cruel. But she was wrong... His hateful remarks were slowly crucifying her.

Wretched, wretched man. She would love to throw something at him, but she could hear her father whisper, "Handle it like a Duchess."

"Then I'll say good night."

She made a detour to the bathroom to brush her teeth. He was still seated at the table drinking the rest of his wine when she passed the kitchen on her way to the stairs.

If he craved his solitude so much, then she would let him have all he wanted. There were several more bottles of wine in the cupboard. He could drink himself into oblivion for all she cared.

The darkness had brought an even heavier mist than last night. Clouds she'd seen in the far horizon had moved much faster than she would have imagined. She shivered involuntarily, glad the boat was moored to the island since there was virtually no visibility at the moment.

By sitting next to the light at the end of the boat, she was able to read. It was almost impossible to concentrate, but she was determined to stay away from Luc until he'd gone to bed and had passed out for the night.

After an hour she noticed the breeze had kicked up. There was a drop in the temperature. Without anything covering her bare legs beneath her shorts, she was starting to get uncomfortable, but she kept on reading.

In another few minutes she felt the first drops of rain. Unable to lie there any longer, she got off the bench with her book and headed for the stairs. No sooner had she passed the kitchen than the lights flickered several times before going out. Great!

Luc must have heard her surprised cry because he

called to her from the cabin. "Did you just shut off the power?"

"No."

"The rain must have shorted out some wiring. I'll take a look at it in the morning. Do you need help coming to bed?"

It was pitch black. "No. Just keep talking and I'll follow your voice."

"Don't move! There's a flashlight in the locker where I found the flare. I'll get it."

But Olivia ignored him and darted across the expanse where she could feel the ladder. In the time it would take him to slide out of bed, she'd climbed beneath the covers of her bunk.

"Olivia?" The alarm in his voice was incredibly satisfying to hear. It proved he wasn't totally devoid of concern for her.

"I'm up here, cozy and warm."

He cursed in French again. "Then stay there! I won't be long."

"Please don't bother with a light tonight," she begged him. "The stairs might be slippery. If you fell and injured yourself after all you've endured, I'd never be able to forgive myself. I'm the reason we're stranded here. This whole situation is my fault," her voice shook.

"In case it's a heavy rain, I need to shut the doors at the top and bottom of the stairs to keep the galley area watertight."

"I'll do that! You get back in bed!"

"For the love of heaven— Can't you once in your hedonistic life think of someone else besides yourself and do as your told?"

Hedonistic? He really saw her as a woman in pursuit of pleasure, devoid of conscience or concern for anyone else?

Hadn't everything she'd done for him today counted for anything?

While she lay there wounded and seething with fresh indignation, she could hear him battening down the hatch.

She prayed he would make it back to bed in one piece. But as soon as she heard him enter the room and get in his bunk, she was waiting for him and leaned her head over the side, armed with a new tactic.

"You're right about me, Luc. I'm not the kind of woman who can be faithful to one man. It isn't in me. I love men too much. I thought I liked Fred and a dozen others before him. Then I met Cesar. It was fun for a while. But then I found myself attracted to his mechanic who wanted to spend time with me after the race."

"Etienne."

"I don't remember his name. If he's the one with the dark blond hair like Fabio, then yes."

"He's married with three children."

"I found that out from one of the other mechanics. Whatever else you may think of me, I draw the line at getting involved with married men. So…I've been thinking about…us."

"Us?" he mouthed the word silkily.

Her heart throbbed so hard in her throat, she almost choked. "Yes. You and me. Since Cesar knows I turned to you, and we're probably not going to make it to Ischia after all, what do you say we take advantage of our situation for the duration of our trip."

''You mean you've decided you're attracted to me now.''

''Well, yes. Strictly on a physical level.''

''Are you that desperate for a man?''

If he happens to be you...

''Not desperate. But we're both here, and we're alone. Why not make these moments as pleasurable as possible. No one else ever has to know.''

She waited to hear his answer. When none was forthcoming, she took it as a yes and scrambled down the ladder with her heart pounding like a jackhammer.

It was taking a gamble, the biggest of her life. But if she could just get him to kiss her, then maybe he would break down enough to admit he loved her. Greer had ended up proposing to Max. Olivia would do the same with Luc. She would confess she was painfully in love with him and wanted to marry him if he would have her. Whatever was in his past, they would deal with it together.

The darkness gave her an edge. She couldn't see Luc's expression, and it seemed to bring her senses alive.

Something told her it wasn't pain that made his breath catch before it turned shallow the second she touched him. The skin on his upper arm felt warm to the touch. It pulsated with life.

This close to his body she breathed in his own male scent. Intoxicated, she leaned over and brushed her lips against his hair-roughened chest. She'd wanted to do this for such a long, long time.

He made no move to touch her back. She didn't mind doing all the work. From the beginning he'd been a challenge. Like a wild stallion that had never known a rope around its neck, he'd put up an enormous fight.

Gentling him was taking time and patience, but she was winning the fight. Even a thoroughbred who ran alone was vulnerable to a little comfort once in a while.

She started to massage his shoulders, marveling at their strength and breadth. "Doesn't this feel good?" she whispered. Being able to play with those corded muscles was ecstasy. A man and a woman had been designed with opposites in mind. Beautiful opposites that were meant to fit together as one pulsating entity.

"Do you have any idea how desirable you are to me?" Unable to resist, she found his chin with her lips. "Um. You have a little beard growing there."

She felt the rasp of his jaw over and over again before her lips slowly moved to his ear. "I love everything about you, Lucien de Falcon. In fact I think I need to take a little bite out of you."

Her teeth grazed his earlobe. She relished the sensation of his hair brushing against her nose. In the next breath she buried her face in its vibrant texture. Maybe it was because she was so blond, but there was something erotic about kissing hair as black as midnight.

Instinct caused her mouth to travel over his forehead to well-formed brows as dark and luxuriant as his hair. "Your eyelashes are tickling my cheek." She smiled before kissing each eyelid, then his aquiline nose. The kind that added a hawk-like quality to his features, denoting his aristocratic Falcon heritage. It set him apart from other men.

"You're the most breathtaking man I've ever known," she confessed. Still on her knees at the side of the bunk, she cradled his face in her hands and started nibbling at the corner of his mouth.

The journey to get this close to Luc had been long and arduous. Almost two months in all. Now that she'd arrived, she intended to take her time and savor what she'd been yearning for.

"I didn't know you had a little scar there," she said when she felt the tiny ridge at the other corner. "It's not visible, but it tells me something about you, even if you won't. So does the tiny nick on your neck."

She kissed both spots again, then closed her mouth fully over his, aching for him to sweep her away. "Darling? Help me out," she begged, feeling feverish at this point.

Just when she was afraid the miracle would never happen, a tremor passed through his powerful body. Suddenly she wasn't doing all the work anymore. His mouth began to respond.

At first it was like the soft, experimental caress of love's first kiss between two young teens who'd been anticipating the moment, yet couldn't quite believe it was really here.

Olivia was running on primal instinct now. Her lips opened of their own accord, unaware of what she was unleashing. Beyond control, all she knew was that the driving force of her desire was coaxing him to take their kiss deeper.

With her mouth fastened on his, she climbed on the mattress, needing to get closer to him. She would be careful not to hurt his leg.

"Finally," she murmured in rapture when she felt his arms close around her. "I've waited so lo—"

Her cry was replaced by little moans because the

startling hunger of his kiss had engulfed her. He caught her to him in an explosion of need. The pleasure was so exquisite she felt it to the tiniest nerve ending in her body.

They moved and breathed together, arms, mouths and bodies locked in a melding as old as time itself. She forgot where she was. Time…place…nothing had any meaning except to go up in flames with the man she loved beyond reason.

Suddenly he shifted her away from him. Caught up in a frenzy of overwhelming passion, she was slow to understand she might have done something to injure him. In a clumsy movement, she rolled off the bed and stood up, but her legs were trembling like jelly.

"Forgive me if I hurt you. I didn't mean to."

"No harm was done," came his answer in a voice devoid of emotion. Without light she couldn't tell what he was thinking, but she sensed a stunning change in him. The blood pounded in her ears.

"What's wrong?"

"Playtime is over."

She weaved on her feet. "I don't understand."

"Of course you do, but a woman like you chooses not to pick up on the signals. I don't recall inviting you to join me in my bed. Because of your history with men, you just assumed you would be welcome.

"Perhaps your 'one for all, all for one' motto is the by-product of being the youngest in a set of triplets, but to be frank, the thought of making love to my brother's latest *pit babe* sickens me. I don't know how I can make myself any clearer than that."

A thousand knives seemed to be stabbing her heart

at once. She held back scalding tears only through the greatest strength of will.

"I don't know, either. How come you didn't push me away sooner?"

"I must admit I was curious to see if there was a conscience hiding somewhere inside that tempting body of yours that would stop you before I did."

Her breath caught. "I noticed you waited until you'd kissed me back first!"

"You're a delicious flavor treat. The trick is to enjoy a small taste rather than to sate one's self with fruit from the basket others have picked over first. When I decide to fully indulge myself, I will pluck the sweetest fruit of my choosing from off the tree and swallow it whole."

Both sisters had warned her Luc wasn't like other men. They were right. His demons were too daunting for her to fight without more information.

But he *had* responded to her.

No man could have kissed her with such soul-destroying intensity if she'd sickened him that much. He would never have let her get that far otherwise.

What she needed was input. The kind only an insider could provide, *if* he was willing...

She climbed back up to her bunk and spent the rest of the torturous night huddled under the covers while she thought out her new plan. Toward morning the elements decided to cooperate. The storm passed over, and the light patter of the rain ceased.

As soon as the first light of dawn filtered into the cabin, she stole out of bed and climbed down the ladder, careful not to make a sound. Luc was in a deep sleep. She could tell by his breathing.

It was vital he stay unconscious for a while longer

since she intended to undo the ropes and start rowing toward the mainland. Her impetuosity had gotten them into this predicament. Now she needed to rely on her ingenuity to get them out on the double quick in order for her latest strategy to work.

She tiptoed to the bathroom. After putting on her bathing suit and T-shirt, she slipped into her sneakers. Quietly opening the doors at the bottom and top of the stairs, she climbed out on a deck still damp from the night's storm. However the mist had lifted enough to give her the visibility she needed.

In a few minutes she'd untied the ropes and had climbed back in the boat. She used the oar to shove off, giving it a hard push for maximum glide. When she couldn't touch bottom anymore, she started paddling, first on one side, then the other.

Within ten minutes every muscle in her body was killing her, but her determination to put her new plan into action had become a driving force. Though progress was slow, even after she got the hang of it, the island had almost disappeared from view. That was a good omen.

She rested for two minutes, then began the back-breaking process all over again.

Within a half hour she'd reached her exhaustion level and sank down on the bench for a breather. That's when she heard the sound of an engine off to the left. Pretty soon she saw a light plane flying over the water. As it came closer, she noticed it had pontoons.

Olivia started jumping up and down, waving her arms.

The plane circled, then landed and taxied toward the boat. A man dove overboard and swam toward the *Gabbiano*. When he reached it and climbed the ladder, she let out a surprised cry.

"Nic! What are you doing here? How did you know we were in trouble?"

His captivating white smile was reassuringly familiar. "Giovanni forgot to tell Fabio that when the wiring gets wet, it causes a short and the power goes off."

She rolled her eyes. "We already found that out last night."

"He called Fabio because he was worried you and Luc might be caught in the storm, so Fabio called me. According to one of the children near the dock, they saw you head east when you left Vernazza.

"Since you girls were so fascinated by Monte Cristo's history on your first trip, I figured it might be your destination. Therefore I instructed the pilot to search this area first."

"Luc and I came across it by accident. Between you and me, the fascination has worn off. It's just a pile of rocks."

He grinned. "Where *is* my cousin?"

"Right here," came Luc's deep, grating voice. Olivia looked over her shoulder and found herself trapped by his enigmatic gaze. "The question is, what are we doing out in the middle of the Mediterranean this time around?"

Nic folded his arms, eyeing both of them with speculation. "I found Señorita Olivo rowing the boat for all she was worth with one oar. That's quite a feat, even for several sailors twice her size and strength."

"I was looking for help."

Luc stood there in cutoffs, disheveled and unshaven, yet hateful as he was, she'd never seen a more attractive man in her life. After being kissed by him last night, after experiencing his embrace if only for a little while, she would never be the same again.

But his grim demeanor reminded her she was a long way from being able to claim victory.

"Well we couldn't just sit on Monte Cristo and do nothing!"

"I'll get the rope attached to the tether," Nic interjected. "We'll tow the boat back to Vernazza for electrical repairs."

Olivia smiled at him. "I've never been in a seaplane before. Are we riding with you?"

"Of course."

"Terrific!"

Ignoring Luc, she climbed up on the side and leaped into the water to make her escape from him.

Within a few minutes she and Luc were seated comfortably behind the pilot and Nic. The seaplane fairly skated across the surface of the water with the *Gabbiano* in tow. While Olivia drank her hot coffee, Nic looked over his shoulder at her.

"What do you think?" No doubt he felt tension emanating from Luc and was trying his best to neutralize it.

"I haven't had this much fun in years. I feel like I'm at Disneyland on one of those children's rides." The two men in front burst into laughter. "This is the only way to see the Riviera. How much would you charge to escort me around on a ten-day trip?"

"More than you could ever afford," Luc muttered, his tone as black as the stubble on his jaw. She couldn't understand his grim disposition. They'd been rescued and he was about to be rid of her. What more did he want from life?

"When I've made my fortune, I'll be able to afford anything I want and I'll buy one of these. In fact I think I'll take flying lessons so I can do everything myself."

"You'll have to sell a lot of rocks first."

"Your encouragement to one who wasn't born being fed by a silver spoon with the Falcon coat of arms does you great credit."

For the rest of the ride back, Olivia pretended Luc hadn't come along. She concentrated instead on the magnificent view of the coastline. The rain had refreshed everything. The greens of the foliage, the pinks and yellows of the flowers were more vivid than usual.

Vernazza was beginning to look like home. The pilot of the seaplane skimmed the harbor in a circle and came to a stop. He'd brought the *Gabbiano* close enough to the pier for some local fisherman to secure it at the end of the dock.

Olivia was first out of her seat. "Nic? Luc shouldn't use his leg anymore today. Last night he strained it unintentionally," she deliberately stated in order to remind him of those moments he wanted to forget. She hoped he was tortured by them. "I'll go aboard and pack up our things."

Pleased when she heard Luc's protest overruled by Nic in no uncertain terms, she dove from the open door into the water and swam for the boat. Once on deck she went below and changed into a blouse and skirt.

After packing both suitcases, she went back up the stairs. Nic had come aboard. He stood by and watched as she reopened her bag and put the pouch of rocks on top of her clothes and toiletries. But when she lowered the lid, it wouldn't close all the way.

He smiled. "Whatever that is, I don't think it's going to fit."

"Yes it will."

She sat down on the lid and that did the trick. Gathering her purse in one hand, she took hold of her suitcase in the other. It weighed a lot more than before, but she didn't mind.

"Let me transport those bags to the plane."

"Only Luc's," she said when Nic started to reach for them. "He's the one who needs to get back to Monaco and rest. Otherwise he'll blame me when it takes his leg longer to heal. I couldn't bear that on my conscience along with everything else."

"Everything else?" Nic shot her a questioning glance.

With her emotions so close to the surface, she was in danger of giving herself away. "I—it was just a figure of speech," she stammered. "I was starting to get nervous out there. Without power I wouldn't have been able to cook us more fish even if I'd been lucky enough to catch another one."

He looked shocked. "You caught fish?"

"Yes. Who would have believed?" She gave him a tired smile. "Thank you for everything, Nic. You've been a real lifesaver."

"Where are you going?" he questioned after she'd kissed his cheek.

"Greer made me promise to take the train to Colorno and spend a few days at Max's villa before I fly home to New York."

It wasn't a lie. Her sister had told her she and Piper

would always have a home with them. They would never have to wait for an invitation.

Of course Olivia had no such intention of traveling to Colorno. There was only one detour she planned to make before leaving Italy, but nobody else needed to know about that, least of all Luc. She just hoped she wasn't too late.

"Bye." With a little wave she stepped off the boat with her suitcase and headed for the town. It was only a five-minute walk to the train station.

"I'd like a one-way ticket to Positano, please."

"Si, signorina."

Before she left for Kingston, she wanted to know why Luc hated her so much. She had a gut instinct the younger Falcon brother could provide her with the answer. Not that it would take away her pain. Nothing could do that, but she wouldn't be able to go on functioning without some kind of explanation.

Nic climbed into the seaplane with the valise. He stashed it behind the seat before his gaze flicked to Luc. "Olivia's not coming."

"Tell me something I don't already know." Luc had seen her march off with her suitcase toward the town, her gleaming blond head held high, her curvaceous body the cynosure of every male eye in the port. "Let's go."

While Nic strapped himself in the co-pilot's seat and told the pilot to take off for Monaco, Luc phoned Signore Galli. The head of security at Genoa airport had dealt with the Duchess sisters before. If Olivia did check in for her overseas flight, the other man would spot her immediately and contact Luc.

Nic didn't try to make further conversation until

they were alone in the back of the limo headed for Luc's house. "Why the call to Signore Galli?"

"If she's flying home from Genoa, I plan to put her on the plane myself. I want proof she has left the continent."

Another experiment like last night and he'd never be able to hold out. The things she'd done to him, the way she'd made him feel... He couldn't believe he'd come so close to being the amoral bastard he'd accused his brother of being. Olivia was poison disguised.

"The sooner thousands of miles separate us, the better."

"I hate to tell you this, but she said she was going to Colorno for a couple of days first."

Luc made an angry sound in his throat. "Neither of her sisters is there which means she lied to you."

"Why would she do that?"

"Because she's probably running to Cesar." In fact he was sure of it. She'd couldn't last twelve hours without a man. "Her next trip on water will probably be a honeymoon cruise. In that case I wish them Godspeed on their way to hell."

A shadow crossed over his cousin's face. "Luc—"

"If you're going to tell me she's not like Genevieve, don't waste your breath. Last night put any doubts about that to rest. I've decided all women are alike, offering themselves to the highest bidder." Even Nina, Nic's deceased fiancée. But that was a secret Luc and Max would take to their graves.

"I think you're mistaken about Olivia."

"You don't know what I know," Luc lashed out, then lowered his head. "Sorry I snapped, but even the most luscious-looking peach can have a rotten pit at its core. Should she end up becoming Madame Cesar de Falcon, how would you like a permanent new neighbor?''

Nic looked stunned. ''You would move to Spain?''

''I can do my engineering anywhere.''

''I think you're getting way ahead of yourself.''

''It's called self preservation, but let's change the subject. I haven't thanked you yet for rescuing us.''

''I was happy to do it, but I must admit your phone call took me by surprise.''

''That storm sneaked up on us.''

''It made the search more difficult. The mist hung in patches out there this morning. I was beginning to get nervous when we couldn't see any sign of the boat. You'll never know my relief when we suddenly found a hole in the clouds and spotted Olivia waving to us.''

''I appreciate your coming. I can always count on you.''

''You've come to my aid more times, but seriously Luc. Though Olivia got you into that mess, you have to give her credit for trying to get you out.''

''Who's side are you on?''

''Yours. Always.''

While they'd been talking, the limo had reached the house and driven into the courtyard. Luc felt for the door handle. ''Let's get inside and eat. I want to hear about your next move to catch our jewel thief.''

''I wish I knew where to start. I need your input.''

Luc's hand tightened on his cane. ''In a few more days I can throw this away. Then I'll be free to drive us wherever the trail leads, unhampered.''

All bad things were finally coming to an end.

CHAPTER SEVEN

By THE time the taxi had deposited Olivia at the foot of some steps leading up the steep cliff to the Varano villa, night had fallen over *Positano*. She asked the driver to wait while she found out if anyone was home.

Though cloud cover hid the sky, it seemed as if all the stars had dipped below it to light up the picturesque town with its cubed-shaped houses built into the sides of two mountain slopes.

Wherever she looked, she had an unexcelled panorama of the Mediterranean bordering the Amalfi Coast.

On the way from the train station the driver charmed her with his account of Hercules, the pagan god of strength who loved a nymph called Amalfi. But she died early, and he buried her in the most beautiful place of the world. To immortalize her, he gave it her name.

How would it feel to be immortalized like that by Luc? The man she loved with every breath in her body...

Her heart heavy, Olivia rang the bell at the side of the door. She didn't have to wait long before a sixtyish-looking housekeeper answered.

"Signorina?"

"Hello. Forgive me for dropping by so late, but I just arrived on the train. My name's Olivia Duchess. I've come to see Cesar. Is he here?"

"Olivia?" a male voice called out from the interior. Suddenly the man in shorts and a T-shirt she'd traveled all this way to visit materialized behind the other woman.

Cesar's curious eyes played over her. "This is an unexpected pleasure. Come in." He bore more than a superficial resemblance to his brother. It caused Olivia's heart to bleed all over again.

"The taxi that brought me here is still waiting below."

"*Bien*. I'll take care of everything while Bianca shows you where to freshen up. Afterward you can join me on the terrace. I was eating supper. After your trip here, I'm sure you must be hungry, too." He disappeared down the steps with the agility of an athlete.

"*Signorina?*"

Olivia followed the housekeeper through the fabulous Mediterranean-styled villa to a guest bathroom. Coming directly from the train it felt good to wash her face and comb her hair.

Feeling a little more presentable, she found Bianca, who walked her out to a veranda filled with flowering plants of every color. Lavender bougainvillea overflowed the balcony. Between the fragrance and the soft night air, the scene was one of enchantment. With the right man...

When Cesar returned she looked up at him from the round glass table where she'd taken a seat. "After putting your life on the line at the track, I can see why you choose to come here to unwind. This is paradise."

He took his place across from her. "You say that with such a tragic look in your eyes, I feel the weight of the world in them. May I offer you something to eat first?'' She shook her head. ''A little wine perhaps?''

''Nothing, thank you. Cesar, please forgive me for bursting in on you like this unannounced. I had no way of knowing whether you were alone, or—''

''I *am* alone, as you can well see.''

She bit her lip. ''The thing is, you have every right to assume why I've come, but it's—''

''It's not because you've been dying of love for me and couldn't stay away from me any longer?'' he broke in with asperity. ''You think I don't know that, *ma belle?*''

Olivia averted her eyes, suddenly feeling like an idiot.

''Contrary to most people's opinion, I'm not quite the shallow fool everyone believes I am, so in love with myself and my love of speed that I imagine the whole world revolves around me and no one else.''

''I never said that,'' she murmured.

''You didn't have to. You were a fan of mine long before you met me. Believing all the hype about me goes with the territory. If I hadn't learned to live with it, I would have gotten out of racing a long time ago.''

So there was a dark side to Cesar, too. Maybe it was inherent in the Falcon genes.

He finished the last of the cheese before eyeing her frankly. ''There's only one person's opinion who truly matters to me besides my parents'. We used to be as close as brothers,'' he said with bitter irony. ''These days he hates my guts.''

She kneaded her hands nervously. ''You're talking about Luc.''

His eyes grew bleak. "Who else? I gather that's why you're here. To talk about him."

"Yes."

"Because you're in love with him."

"Yes."

"And he's being difficult."

Olivia almost choked on the word.

"I can see that he is," Cesar drawled. "Where do you want to start?"

"At the beginning."

He threw his arm over the back of his chair. "In the beginning, there was Luc. My hero. I wanted to be like him, do everything he did. But he was brilliant in math, fantastic at any sport, and could have any woman he wanted without even thinking about it.

"I on the other hand was a late bloomer who struggled in school, was only passable at most sports, and believe it or not, was scared of women."

"That's how it was with me and Greer," Olivia blurted. "She was the oldest. The smart one with all the ideas. She could do anything! She had so much confidence. Men adored her. I...worshiped her."

Cesar eyed her with compassion. "We're both victims of the youngest-child syndrome."

She nodded.

"One day Luc and our cousins took me to a Formula I race with them. Though Luc had no interest in being a competitor, it was a sport my brother loved to watch.

"When the winner of the Grand Prix walked up to the podium to collect his prize, I saw admiration in Luc's eyes. That was an electrifying moment for me. I decided I would learn to race cars so that Luc would admire *me* like that one day.

"Over the years the sport has been good to me, and with all the endorsements, I've been able to invest in several businesses."

Cesar had been leading up to something important. "But Luc didn't admire you?"

"On the contrary. He backed me, went to most of my races. Supported me when mother wanted me to quit racing before I got killed."

"Then what happened to change everything?"

His expression became a study in pain, reminding her so much of Luc she groaned.

"Her name was Genevieve Leblanc."

Olivia's heart pounded out a nonstop tattoo.

"She came to the Cote D'Azur from Toulon, looking for work. He hired her to be a secretary for the company he'd started up. One thing led to another and they got engaged."

Of course Luc had had girlfriends. But the knowledge that he'd had a fiancée hit Olivia as if she'd been dealt a physical blow.

"How long ago was this?"

"Almost two years to the day."

She shifted in the chair. Taking her courage in her hands she asked, "Why aren't they married, Cesar?"

He unexpectedly pushed himself away from the table and stood up. "A month before their wedding, Luc had to fly to the States for a special robotics engineering conference. I was in Monza racing and came in third. To my surprise, Genevieve showed up to lend her support while Luc was away.

"It surprised me even more when she insisted on coming back here to Positano, allegedly to cheer me up and enjoy a little vacation from the frantic wedding preparations.

"I told her to make herself comfortable. Then I excused myself. You see, after a race there's a routine I always follow to restore me.

"Strapped in the car like an astronaut, you start to feel claustrophobic. To help me unwind, I get on my dirt bike and push myself physically through the mountain roads here until I've worn myself out. After a swim in the ocean, I fall into bed and sleep for ten to twelve hours without dreams.

"However this time when I got under the covers, I discovered I wasn't alone."

At this point Olivia slid off the chair and walked over to the railing, needing to cling to something.

"No one will ever know the horror I felt. Disgust drove me to the bathroom where I was literally sick. When I returned to the bedroom, she was still there with a smile on her face. She said she thought I understood she was attracted to me, and was positive I reciprocated her feelings.

"She said a lot of things, the upshot being that Luc never had to know. It would be our secret. Then she urged me to come to bed."

A moan came out of Olivia.

"I told her I loved my brother more than my own life. If she didn't tell him what she'd done, then I would. In the next breath I threw her out and told her I never wanted to see her again.

"A few days later, Luc returned from the conference. I was summoned to the family villa where he'd gathered our parents together. He informed us there wasn't going to be a wedding after all. Heartsick as I was for him, I was thankful the truth had come out.

"Later that evening I took Luc aside to talk to him

about everything. To my shock he said there wasn't anything to talk about. It was over.''

Olivia swung toward him. ''He never let you explain what happened?'' she cried.

''No. A wall had gone up between us. Our relationship has never been the same since.''

''But she could have told him any lie she wanted, and probably did!''

Cesar's eyes were alive with pain. ''True. Still, Luc had grown up with me and knew me. He had to know I loved him too much to ever betray him like that. I would have done anything for him.''

''Then she must have painted a picture that made it impossible for him to figure out the truth without help.''

''You're right, but he never gave me the chance. In the two years since his breakup with Genevieve, the only thing he has ever asked of me was to show up on the *Piccione* to meet you after the Grand Prix. I was overjoyed because I thought it meant he'd finally worked it out and realized she'd been the one to blame.''

''So you took me behind the scenes of the racing world in order to get back in your brother's good graces?''

''Yes. But it was no penance, believe me.''

She swallowed hard. ''Thank you for your honesty.''

He gave her a sheepish glance. ''You may not thank me when I tell you everything I did.''

''What do you mean?''

''From the moment he called me and asked me to meet the two of you on the boat, I knew instinctively you'd become someone important to him.''

She shook her head. "He felt an obligation to me after the horrible way he and your cousins treated us when they thought we were the jewel thieves."

"No, Olivia. Something happened aboard the *Piccione* that changed him. In one sense I was thrilled to think he could have feelings for another woman again. But in another, I was nervous because you showed such an eagerness to get to know me. Especially when you knew all my racing statistics. After the history with Genevieve, I had to proceed carefully."

"I didn't know!" she cried again in anguish. "When I couldn't get him to respond to me, I played up to you in order to make him jealous. It was the worst thing I could have done, but then I'm known for getting myself into the worst messes possible."

One corner of his mouth lifted. "I finally figured that out at the wedding. When I heard you two fighting, I decided to help nature along by inviting you to come to Monza with me."

"You invited me on purpose? I mean, not because you were interested in me?"

"I could have been very interested if I'd met you before he did. But to answer your question, I decided to test you in the only way I knew how."

Her eyes grew huge. "So that business about buying me a ring—"

"Was the carrot I dangled to see if you would go for the bait. A test if you like to prove your worthiness to marry my brother."

"Cesar—" Her mind was reeling.

"Not only did you laugh at me, you refused to let me really kiss you. I knew then you loved him heart and soul."

"I do!" She clapped her hands to her cheeks. "So *that's* what you meant on the phone when you said you hoped he would realize it."

He nodded. "You'll never know how happy I was to find out you'd gone straight to his house after you left Monza. I took it as a foregone conclusion that by now the two of you would be announcing your own wedding plans." He cocked his head. "How come you're here instead of at the villa with him?"

"Oh, Cesar—I'm in the worst trouble imaginable. He hates me. He really hates me. After everything you've told me, now I know why. I think maybe too much damage has been done."

"Tell me what happened after our phone call."

Without stopping for breath she blurted everything. It was a relief to be able to unburden herself to someone who loved Luc as much as she did.

"When he said the thought of making love to one of his brother's pit babes sickened him, I knew his pain had to be tied up to you in some way. I was such a fool to throw myself at him like that. But nothing else seemed to be working. I thought if I could just break him down a little, then I'd propose to him.

"My greatest worry now is, even if I could get him to listen to reason, he would probably accuse me of wanting to get married on the rebound just because Greer has a husband and I'm at a loose end."

Cesar grinned. "Knowing my brother's engineering brain, that thought has probably crossed his mind already. It's even possible he believes you've picked him because he's Max's cousin and you'll do anything to keep up with your older sister."

Olivia looked stricken. "I hadn't thought of that! He's a very complicated man."

He stared at her through veiled eyes. "The best ones are. I love him. The accident he survived was a blow he didn't need after the emotional devastation of Genevieve's betrayal. He deserves all the happiness life has to give him."

She hung her head. "I don't know what to do. I know what I *should* do. Greer would tell me to go straight home and forget him."

"What do you want to do?" he asked softly.

"Find the path to his heart, but I don't think there's a way."

"After getting up at the crack of dawn to row the *Gabbiano* by yourself to find help, you're too tired to think straight. I'll ask Bianca to show you to one of the guest bedrooms.

"Sometimes when I've exhausted every idea to ace out an opponent on the track, a good night's sleep restores me and I come up with a killer strategy."

She bit her lip. "It would have to be that good to make a dent in his armor."

"The Duchess triplets have a reputation for doing the impossible under the most improbable circumstances. If you can't figure out a way to get to my brother, then it can't be done."

"I think I'm crazy about you, Cesar de Falcon."

"Now she tells me!"

While they smiled at each other with a perfect understanding, Olivia heard Cesar's cell phone go off. His gaze flicked to hers. "My bet it's big brother trying to find out where you are because he can't stand the suspense any longer. What do you want me to tell him?"

Her heart was racing. ''What does your caller ID say?''

He pulled it out of his pocket to look. ''It's Max.''

Olivia didn't know whether to be glad or devastated. She watched Cesar click on. As soon as he'd said *ciao*, he handed her the phone. ''It's Greer,'' he mouthed the words.

Not again—

She turned her back on Cesar. ''How did you know I was here?'' she demanded of her sister in a hushed tone.

''Maybe because I've lived with you for twenty-seven years and know exactly how your mind works,'' Greer whispered back. ''Olivia Duchess—don't you know you've done the worst thing you could ever do to run straight to Cesar? Any hope you might have had with Luc has flown straight out the window!''

Olivia couldn't stand it when her sister was right, which was ninety-nine percent of the time. ''You're supposed to be on your honeymoon instead of minding my business.''

''I'm afraid your getting involved with the Falcon brothers has made this all our business! Piper phoned Nic because she was desperate to know where you were.

''You promised to phone her and you never did! She thought you were going to fly home from Genoa, but Nic said you were taking the train to Colorno. When she called there, the maids reported that you never arrived, so she phoned Nic who phoned Max to find out if we knew anything. Piper's frantic!''

''I couldn't call her. Luc and I were marooned on Monte Cristo without a phone.''

"That's not true, Olivia! You know very well Luc had one with him, otherwise how would Nic have known to come and rescue you, let alone *where* to find you!"

Olivia's blue eyes rounded in wonder.

Luc had his cell phone with him the whole time?

Then that meant he'd hidden it...

And that meant he hadn't wanted to be rescued yet, which meant—

Excitement charged her body like a bolt of lightning. This changed everything!

"Thank you for calling me, Greer. I promise to phone Piper right away. Give my love to Max. Enjoy the rest of your honeymoon."

"Olivi—"

She clicked off.

"Is everything all right?" Cesar inquired.

She whirled around and handed him the phone. "Everything's fine! Cesar? Will you do me a favor?" Her plan *had* to work.

"*Bien sûr.* Anything."

"Walk me to the foyer and call for Bianca. When she comes so she can be a witness, tell me to get out of your house."

"*Comment?* What did you say?" he asked incredulously.

"Please just do it? Tell me to leave the premises immediately or you'll call the police and have me arrested for trespassing."

Recognition suddenly dawned in his blue-gray eyes. "Ah—you are up to one of your famous Duchess tricks."

She bit her lip. "You won't give me away?"

He crossed his heart.

Getting into his part, he grabbed hold of her arm and dragged her into the foyer, calling out in a loud, urgent voice for Bianca as he did so. The housekeeper came running.

"Bianca? Please bring Mademoiselle Duchess's suitcase back. I want her out of this house and gone within two minutes or I am calling for the police."

When he shook Olivia off, almost causing her to stumble because he didn't know his own strength, the older woman gasped before hurrying away to do his bidding.

Taking advantage of her absence, Cesar kissed Olivia's cheek. "*Bonne chance, ma belle,* but I don't think you will need it because you have a way of making your own luck.

"When you reach the first turn in the road below the villa, wait there and a taxi will be along shortly to take you wherever you wish to go."

"Thank you, Cesar. Whether my plan works or not, I want you to know you're wonderful." She gave him a hug before he disappeared, leaving her to face the loyal housekeeper who dropped the suitcase at her feet the way she was supposed to do.

"You heard, Cesar. Go!" She made a violent gesture with her hands.

"I'm leaving, even if he misunderstood my intentions."

The older woman wagged an index finger in front of her. "He does not misunderstand why a woman comes to his house this late at night alone. The only woman he will ever have in this house will be his wife!"

"But I came to talk to him about Luc. Luc's the one I love."

"Then you find my poor Luca and tell *him*. There was trouble in this house once before," she muttered, probably revealing more than she meant to. "And stay away from my poor Cesar. They have both suffered enough!"

"I agree. Thank you for your hospitality, Bianca," she said before closing the door.

By the time she made it to the horseshoe bend in the road with her suitcase, a taxi was waiting for her.

"Thank you for coming."

The driver nodded. "*Si, signorina.* Signore di Falcone told me to take you wherever you wish to go."

"Naples airport. I have to get to Nice before morning."

"*Bene.*"

No telling what Luc's plans were. Even though he was supposed to be resting his leg, he might have gone to his parents' home—or to Nic's in Spain.

She hoped not the latter. Any more travel tonight was anathema to her. Besides, she needed to be alone with Luc.

Four hours later another taxi dropped her off in the courtyard of Luc's villa. At five-fifteen in the morning, it was still dark. She paid the driver and got out with her suitcase in hand. To be certain she wasn't stranded, she asked him to wait.

Here we go again.

She walked up to the door and rang the bell. Luc had told her he employed staff during the weekdays, so she expected a maid to answer. When no one came, she pressed the button and didn't let up.

Pretty soon she heard cursing.

A smile broke out on her face. She turned to the taxi driver. "You can go."

By the time Luc opened the door wearing the bottom half of a pair of sweats, all she could see were two red taillights disappearing from the courtyard.

"Surprise, surprise. I'm *baaaack.*" She stepped over his cane and walked in carrying her suitcase.

She probably looked as messy as she felt still dressed in the same skirt and blouse she'd been wearing when he'd last seen her. Everything needed laundering.

Not daring to look at him for fear his expression would terrify her she said, "Sorry to wake you, but now that I'm here you can go back to bed. I know the way to my room."

Without a second's hesitation, she trudged up the staircase to the yellow room she'd chosen for her own. It was heaven to walk in the en suite bathroom and disrobe, anticipating a hot shower.

There'd been too many boat, train and plane rides in one day. She stood under the spray and let the water wash away the grime before she worked the shampoo into a lather.

This was pure luxury. When she wandered into the bedroom a few minutes later with her hair and body wrapped in two fluffy towels, she discovered Luc standing inside the doorway watching her. He was too far away for her to see the look in his eyes. It was just as well she couldn't.

"I don't have anything clean to wear. Do you think you could lend me a T-shirt while I put in a wash?"

"There's a robe in the closet." His voice sounded like it had come from a dark cavern, but so far he hadn't made a move to throw her out yet. A good sign.

She opened the door to the walk-in closet and found a fleece robe in pale blue hanging on a hook. After putting it on and cinching the belt around her slender waist, she emerged with both towels draped over her arm.

"It's lovely. Thank you for your hospitality. I'll wash my clothes after I've had a good six hours of sleep. Then I'll feel like a new person." She tossed the towels over the back of a chair and climbed under the covers of the bed. "Good night."

She rolled on her side so her back was facing him.

When he turned off the light, she assumed he was either too exhausted or too enraged, or maybe both, to deal with her until tomorrow. But in that regard, she turned out to be dead wrong. The side of the bed gave right behind her.

"What do I have to do to get rid of you?"

If she hadn't known he'd purposely lied to her about the phone—if he hadn't covered her mouth with a hunger equal to her own, his question would have driven her away for good.

"You still owe me a Riviera trip. All you have to do is call someone to fit the *Gabbiano* with a new sail and repair the short in the wiring. When I wake up, I'll get us packed and we'll fly back to Vernazza. We can buy some books and groceries at the port."

"That's all I have to do," he murmured with quiet menace.

"Well, there might be some other things, but I'd rather you surprised me. Oh—there is one thing—"

She turned over and found herself wedged against his hip. "We'll need to stop by the hospital first to get your phone. We don't want to go off this time without it. You know. In case something else goes wrong and we're stranded.

"It was just plain lucky Giovanni remembered about the wiring and called Fabio. We were down to a couple of eggs and one plum. We might not be so lucky again."

He didn't move a muscle, but she saw something flicker in the silvery recesses of his eyes illuminated by the light from the hall.

"Where have you been today?" he demanded.

"Here and there."

"What in the hell does that mean?"

"Sometimes at home when I'm upset, I ride the subway to the end of the line and back while I think."

"You were upset?"

"Well naturally. Our trip turned out to be a fiasco, and I'd had my heart set on it."

She heard a sharp intake of breath. "So you rode the train to the end of the line and back, is that it?"

"More or less."

"That must have been some ride."

"It was. I met at least fifty playboys who all wanted to show me the time of my life if I would let them."

His lips thinned to a white line. "So why didn't you take one of them up on his offer?"

"The kind of playboy I'm looking for owns the train, he doesn't ride on it."

"You wouldn't by any chance have ridden as far as Positano—" He left the sentence hanging in the air.

"Since you know I did, why don't you just be honest about it and ask me if Cesar and I went shopping for a ring? But then you already know the answer to that question because I wouldn't be here banging on your door if we were celebrating our engagement.''

"What's the matter? Wasn't he home?"

Tired of the sneer in his tone she said, "Oh, he was there all right."

"And?"

"It was a sobering experience. I'd only gone there to talk to him about you because you gave me permission. He turned on me just like you did and told me to get out!"

"You're lying."

"If you don't believe me, ask Bianca. She dumped my suitcase at my feet, muttering something about how much her poor Luca and her poor Cesar had suffered.

"I ended up having to walk to town from the villa at one o'clock in the morning carrying my suitcase, which was so heavy my arm still aches." She hoped one little lie wouldn't make her a horrible person.

"I warned you those rocks might turn out to be a weight around your neck."

"At least they're not as heavy as the burden you and Cesar carry in your hearts."

Luc suddenly got up from the bed, taking away the warmth of his solid frame. "What in blazes are you talking about?"

Talking about Cesar had been a calculated risk on her part.

"Grief. I'm no stranger to it, either. What you need is a little cheering up. How about teaching me how to sail? You could lie on deck to rest your leg and bark out instructions. I'll do all the work. I'd like to take some good memories back to New York with me. They're going to have to last a long time.''

He rubbed the back of his neck. ''You have a sister living in Italy you can visit any time you want.''

''That's the whole point. Greer needs her space with Max. He doesn't want to be married to triplets, so Piper and I aren't planning to descend on her more than once a year.''

''I thought you were on the hunt for a Riviera playboy. A once a year visit's going to cut down on your window of opportunity.''

''That's all right. Greer caught hers. One out of three isn't bad. Besides, I've got a new Internet business to run. But I don't want to think about work while I'm on vacation. It shouldn't take that long to repair the boat, right?

''However if the thought of being with me sickens you so much, I'll go to Vernazza and hire someone to take me sailing on the *Gabbiano*. Since you owe me, I'll put it on your bill. Now if you don't mind, I need some sleep, so I would appreciate it if you would turn out the hall light.''

CHAPTER EIGHT

"Nic? Are you awake?"

Luc heard a groaning sound come over the phone line. "I am now. Another emergency must have come up for you to call at six in the morning."

"Emergency—catastrophe— You name it."

"I take it we're talking about Olivia."

He closed his eyes tightly. "She's back."

"As in—"

"As in under my roof, using my shower, sleeping in the bedroom next to mine." The sight of her in that towel would haunt him forever.

"When did this happen?"

"An hour ago."

"Where's she been?"

"I'll give you one guess."

"Then— "

"Don't ask—" Luc cut him off. "I'm not going to be able to get rid of her until she's taken her damn boat trip. Fabio will know someone who could repair the wiring and put up a new sail today. But I need you to crew for us."

"You don't need me when you've got Olivia. She could do it if you showed her how."

He grimaced. "That's her plan."

A sound of exasperation came out of Nic. "If you really don't want to be with her, why did you let her in the door?"

"You know why. She's Greer's sister. If I offend

her too deeply, it will end up affecting Max. That's the last thing I want to see happen.''

''Point taken.''

''The way I figure it, if we follow her original itinerary, let her have her fun, she'll finally go home. Then we can get back to business as usual.''

After a long silence, ''You want a fully loaded boat?''

''That's the idea. Let's not give her anything to complain about. I'll do the cooking while you play captain.''

''Just like old times.''

''Not quite,'' Luc murmured. ''This time she won't be trying to run away. If there's one good thing to come of this, a few more days rest and I won't ever need the cane again. At that point I can leave her in your capable hands for the rest of the trip. You don't mind seeing her off on the plane in Malaga, do you?''

''You know better than to ask that question. I'll get packed and take off for Vernazza.''

Luc knew he was asking a lot of his cousin, but this was one time when he had no other choice. Being alone in this house with Olivia was bad enough. Being alone with her on the *Gabbiano* was out of the question. What he needed was the gift of forgetfulness, but there was no such animal.

I've been thinking about…us.

Us?

Yes. You and me. Since Cesar knows I turned to you, and we're probably not going to make it to Ischia after all, what do you say we take advantage of our situation for the duration of our trip.

Luc's lungs constricted because he would never know what really went on between her and his brother. Even if they hadn't made love, she'd nursed a passion for Cesar long before she'd met Luc.

Heaven help him, how long until he stopped caring?

"Nic?"

"Yes?"

Luc expelled the breath he'd been holding. "Thank you. You know what I'm trying to say."

"I do. Without you and Max, I'd never have made it this far. We'll talk later."

After they'd hung up, Luc placed a call to Fabio who told him not to worry. The repairs would be done by late afternoon.

With that settled, he went back to bed. Unfortunately his sleep was sporadic and fitful, denying him the one temporary panacea for the blackness that had descended with a vengeance since Olivia's arrival.

Another three days of torment loomed ahead of him. Three days where he couldn't hibernate in order to banish certain images from his mind.

Thank heaven for Nic who would be there to help him fight this sickness.

Like Max, Luc had caught the Duchess virus, but unlike his cousin, he'd developed serious complications for which there was no cure.

After another half hour of tossing and turning, he got up to shower and shave. He was just coming back in the bedroom to get dressed when he heard the doorbell ring.

He glanced at his watch. It was ten after ten. Whoever it was, one of the staff would get it, or so he thought. When the bell rang again and again, he suddenly remembered he'd given his help the rest of the week off.

Whoever it was didn't plan on going away any time soon.

Throwing on his robe, he started for the stairs with his cane. Halfway down he caught sight of Olivia's long, beautiful legs. She was still dressed in the blue robe and had already opened the door.

"Madame Falcon—"

Hell. That was all he needed.

"*Bonjour, mademoiselle.* Is my son here?"

"I'm here, *maman.*"

She entered the house. "Don't come the rest of the way, *mon fils.* I only dropped by to see how your leg was doing."

His elegant, black-haired mother eyed him with concern, acting for all the world as if she wasn't shocked to discover one of Greer's sisters on the premises.

With those cheeks a warm pink, and her golden curls in alluring disarray, Olivia looked as if she'd just left Luc's bed. No doubt it was the same way she'd looked in the dark the night before last when he'd come close to devouring her, all rosy skin and succulent flesh.

Somehow he'd stopped short of taking the last bite. He would have consumed a pit that would have filled his soul with bitterness.

"He's on it way too much," his nemesis spoke up before Luc could. "I'm afraid I'm to blame for that. Last night, or should I say at five this morning, I arrived on his doorstep, having just come from visiting Cesar."

Olivia had his mother's attention now.

"How is my younger son?"

"I'll tell you all about him in a minute. Why don't you go upstairs with Luc and I'll bring some tea and rolls. I discovered Luc had given his staff a few days off so I volunteered to wait on him."

"That's very kind of you."

"Not at all. It's the least I can do to reciprocate. Your sons are the greatest hosts in the world, something they learned growing up with such a wonderful mother. Between Cesar showing me the racing world, and Luc taking me sailing, I've been having the time of my life and can't bear for it to end," she added before disappearing.

Luc shouldn't have been surprised a woman with no scruples would make a comment like that to his mother.

"The Duchess triplets are so charming, aren't they?" Once they reached his room she grasped his face in her hands and kissed him on both cheeks. "I'm glad someone's here to take care of you this morning. Now lie down and put your leg up."

She took the cane from him and rested it against the end table while he got back in bed. "The first thing I want to know is, what did the doctor say about your progress?"

"My leg will never be as good as new, but in three more days I won't have to use a prop anymore."

Her eyes glistened with tears. "One of my prayers has been answered anyway."

Luc averted his eyes, aware his mother agonized over the fact that neither he nor Cesar had settled down yet. Ever since Max announced his engagement in June she'd been making maternal noises. It had only heightened the tension already existing between him and Cesar.

"Here we are."

His uninvited houseguest entered his bedroom carrying a tray with everything needed to enjoy a delicious breakfast. No surprise there, either. Olivia was a woman equally at home in the kitchen as the bedroom.

She set it down on the coffee table between the two love seats. "Please excuse me for answering the door in this guest robe, Madame Falcon. I'm washing my clothes as we speak. The *Gabbiano* didn't have a washer or dryer."

"The *Gabbiano*?"

Luc groaned. "It's Giovanni's boat, *maman*. The *Piccione* wasn't available."

"It's not a problem," Olivia assured his mother.

She served them a plate of rolls and tea, then poured a cup for herself and came to stand next to the bed where his mother was seated next to him.

"Right now the boat is getting a new sail and the wiring's being fixed so I can enjoy what's left of my holiday. But before Luc tells you about us being caught in a storm, you were anxious to hear how Cesar is doing."

"I'm always anxious about him. He hasn't been home since his win."

This was one time when Luc's mother was better off not knowing what went on behind the scenes. But it was as if Olivia could read Luc's mind because in the next breath she said, "I don't pretend to know a great deal about your sons, but from what little I've seen, they crave their down time away from the masses."

Shut up, Olivia.

His mother had forgotten he was in the room. "What do you mean?"

"Cesar sits alone on his terrace high above Amalfi's resting place, while Luc contemplates the world from this eyrie. It must come from being born on a hillside."

His mother chuckled. "Their father is the same. He feels claustrophobic without a view to look down upon. You're very observant."

"So is Bianca. She fusses around Cesar like a grandmother with a beloved grandson. It was very touching the way she tried to protect him from me."

She blinked. "From you?"

Olivia smiled. "Yes. Cesar told me he always spends a week there after a race and assured me the door would be open if I wanted to visit before I left for the States. I thought with the *Gabbiano* in for repairs, I would take a train ride and drop in on him.

"But when Bianca answered the door, she had no idea I was a cousin-in-law of sorts through marriage to Luc and Cesar. She thought I was one of the women from the track who flings themselves headlong at Cesar. Apparently it's an occupational hazard."

"It's disgusting."

"I couldn't agree more. Especially since Cesar had already confided to me that a woman engaged to one of his best friends showed up at the villa a couple of years ago uninvited and caused him real grief."

The croissant Luc had been eating fell to his plate.

"He never said anything about that to his father or me."

"I don't imagine that's something he would want

anyone to know about. He's too much of a gentleman to hurt his friend. Bianca was witness to the whole thing and kept his secret. But I understand she's been his self-appointed watchdog ever since.''

"Good for her!''

"I agree. That's why it didn't bother me when she practically threw my suitcase at me on my way out.''

"She was that rude to you?''

"I didn't mind. In fact I admired her loyalty. Before she slammed the door, she informed me that the only woman who would ever be allowed to spend the night at the villa with Cesar would be his wife.''

"His father and I live in hope he'll meet the right person one day.''

"He will. Right now he's doing everything he can to be successful at what he does best. It's hard when you're the younger sibling.''

Damn if that tremor in her voice didn't sound genuine to Luc.

"What do you mean, my dear?''

"Luc is like my sister Greer. You know. Perfect.''

While Luc sat there in shock, his mother patted Olivia's hand. "Ah, you miss her. Of course you do being a triplet.''

"No one was ever good enough for her until Max came along.''

"I've never seen my nephew so happy.''

"Mother and Daddy would have adored him.''

"You must miss them very much, too.''

"You can't imagine. Luc and Cesar are so lucky to have you.''

On cue, Luc's mother turned to look at him. "Did you hear that, *mon fils*?''

Luc had already rolled out of the other side of the bed. "I heard, *maman*."

He'd heard something else, too. Until he could talk to Cesar alone, he would have no peace. But before he came face to face with his brother, he needed to be able to stand on his own two feet without help.

"If you're through eating, I'll take the tray and give you some time alone. Ask Luc to tell you about our trip to Monte Cristo."

"That dreary place?"

He shut the door to the bathroom on the rest of their conversation.

Vernazza took on a pinkish glow at sunset. Even Olivia felt bathed in it as she jumped down from the helicopter. Her gaze automatically flew to the pier. To her joy a sail not yet unfurled had been attached to the mast of the *Gabbiano*.

With the wiring fixed, she was getting a second chance for her dream trip of a lifetime with Luc. Just the two of them sailing the high seas.

The first time aboard the *Piccione* didn't count, not with her sisters and Luc's cousins around.

Olivia refused to let his vile mood dampen her spirits. Since his mother's unexpected visit, he'd been more unapproachable than usual. Instead of flinging scathing retorts at her meant to injure, he'd chosen not to talk unless absolutely necessary.

She hoped to heaven it meant the things she'd let drop about her visit to Cesar's were eating him alive. Surely at some point he would be driven to learn the truth for himself. But maybe that was wishful thinking.

Olivia had taken a terrible risk discussing painful,

private family issues with his mother. Luc might never forgive her for it, but it was that or walk away from him. Her jaw hardened. That was something she couldn't do.

As before, she carried both suitcases and paced her steps to his. When they drew closer, she spied a lot of things on deck that hadn't been there before; a sun mattress, water skis, snorkeling gear, deck chairs and a lounger.

She let out a sound of delight.

"I take it you're pleased."

"I'm delighted." She lowered the suitcases into the boat before getting in herself. Luc moved too fast for her to help him down. She assumed his medication had dulled his pain for the moment.

"Why don't you stretch out on that lounger and tell me what to do first? I'd like to sail for a while along the coast before we have to put in at the next port."

He cocked one black eyebrow. "You don't want to get settled in first?"

"We already ate an early dinner, and there'll be time to unpack later."

"Give me a minute to go below then."

"Okay. Hurry."

His mouth twisted into a strange smile before he disappeared down the stairs. She didn't know what to make of it. Maybe beneath the casement of ice beat a heart that was excited to be alone with her, too, but he would never own up to it.

Olivia hugged her arms to her waist and looked all around, soaking in the atmosphere. This was her last chance to work on him.

Earlier in the day while Luc slept, she'd gone shopping to buy some sleepwear and a few casual outfits. The white cargo pants and aqua top she'd put on were perfect for evening when the temperature turned cooler.

Just before they'd left the villa, she'd phoned Piper who was still in bed at the apartment in Kingston. Afraid her sister would try to discourage her from taking this trip, Olivia didn't give her a chance to talk.

Instead she explained she and Luc were on their way out the door, and she'd call her again in a couple of days. After telling her she loved her, Olivia hung up the phone, relieved to have touched base with Piper without letting it turn into a frustrating exchange.

A few fishermen walked past, calling out to her in Italian. Words like *bellissima*. She smiled and waved back.

It reminded her of the evening she and her sisters had run away from Luc and his cousins on their newly purchased bikes. Every male along the road had whistled and shouted at them. But she'd only wanted Luc's attention. No one else's.

Now she was alone with him. Nothing compared to the feelings alive inside of her at this very moment.

"*Señorita Olivo?* It's time to set sail for Monterosso. Are you ready for your first lesson?"

Olivia's heart did a nosedive that went straight through the floor of the boat.

She'd heard that voice before. Yesterday morning in fact. It was as familiar as Luc's. Not that she didn't like Nic. He was awesome. But his presence could only mean one thing...

Don't let him know how you feel. Don't let either

*of them know. She would beat Luc at his game if it
killed her!*

She turned around with a beatific smile on her face.
Luc had come back up on deck with him.

"Nic—what a fabulous surprise! I'm so glad
you're here. Can you be with us the whole trip?"

"Of course. I've cleared my calendar of business
so I could come on this holiday, too. We'll sail all
the way to Marbella where you will be a guest at my
house for a change."

"Terrific!" She ran over and gave him an enthu-
siastic hug in front of Luc who by this time had
stretched out on the lounger. She beamed up at his
cousin. "This will be perfect. Now I have someone
to enjoy the nightlife with me."

His brown eyes gleamed. "You like dancing?"

"I adore it. This is turning out much better than
I'd dared hope," she replied in all honesty as visions
of new possibilities to provoke Luc filled her mind.
"Your presence relieves me of a worry."

"You should have no worries on vacation!"

"It's just that I promised your aunt I'd take good
care of her son on this trip. With you along as captain
of the *Gabbiano,* nothing can go wrong."

"You didn't always think that." He grinned.

She grinned back. "A lady is known to change her
mind."

Nic chuckled. "We'll spell each other off helping
Luc."

"Absolutely. But right now I want my first sailing
lesson."

"Anything to please one of Max's sisters-in-law.
I'd like to stay in his good graces if you know what
I mean."

"That works both ways, Nic. I want to be the kind of sister-in-law he admires so he'll never wish we weren't related." *Unlike someone else she knew.*

"Max would never wish that."

"Piper's so worried about interfering, she says she won't be coming to Europe again except for the christening of their first child. Unless Max and Greer decide to adopt, that won't be happening."

A frown broke out on his face. "Señorita Piper said that?"

"Yes. I'm afraid she was born with enough angst for the three of us. It's the *artiste* in her. She has a conscience that works overtime."

Just then Olivia made the mistake of allowing her eyes to stray to Luc's. He was staring at her as if to say that explained why Olivia didn't have a trace of one.

"I believe it's the middle child syndrome," she continued to explain to Nic. "Piper's the peacemaker."

Nic's brows formed a distinct bar. "It won't please Max if she stays away from Greer with the result that his wife is upset."

"But Piper sees it as doing Max a favor. When he makes remarks about the three of us being joined in a seamless line, she doesn't think he's teasing. Frankly, neither do I."

He eyed her with speculation. "How is Piper handling being alone?"

Was that an idle question, or was there something more significant behind his query? Olivia decided to find out.

"Oh, she's not alone. Tom could hardly wait for her to get back from the wedding."

The silence following her remark spoke volumes. So did his next question. "Shall we set sail? You'll find a life jacket in the locker behind you."

She turned to get it and put it on, aware of Luc's silvery gaze following her every movement. "Your first mate is ready."

Nic flashed her that stunning Castilian smile that masked many secrets. "All right. Untie the ropes, then report to the mast."

"Aye Aye, sir."

They worked in harmony. He started the engine. The *Gabbiano* moved smoothly out of the harbor to open water.

"Feel that breeze?"

She nodded.

"Here comes your first lesson."

Nic was a master teacher. Within a few minutes she'd undone the sail the way he'd told her. The wind took over the rest, filling it until it resembled a fat pillow. She almost fell as the boat listed and shot forward.

They were moving without the aid of the engine. Though Olivia was devastated to think Luc hadn't wanted to be alone with her, she couldn't help but cry out from the sheer exhilaration of knifing through the water toward the fading light in the west.

"What do you think?" Nic called to her.

She lifted her face to experience the full effect of the salt spray. "I'm in heaven!"

So was Nic. She could tell by his exultant laugh. Out of the periphery she noticed Luc glowering.

The steady breeze drove them as if by an unseen hand. It was love at the first lunge for Olivia. "I feel like a dolphin or a tuna!"

He laughed harder and she joined him. Too soon he pointed to some lights along the coast. "Monterosso!"

"Already?"

"You want to go on to the next town?"

"No! I want to see everything!"

"Then you shall!" he assured her before taking over. With the greatest of expertise he brought them around to the port. The town sparkled like a woman's diamond tiara.

Once they reached the buoys, he folded up the sail and they glided to the shore where a lot of other boats had anchored for the night.

She could hear music and voices. People were out swimming, playing on the beach.

Olivia couldn't wait to join them. She'd put on her bikini ahead of time. It only took her a minute to fling off her top and pants.

"I'll be back!" she called over her shoulder. Ignoring Luc's muttered imprecation, she got up on the side of the boat and dove in.

The cool water couldn't have been more inviting. It grew warmer nearer the sand. Olivia swam around, floating on her back so she could take in the view.

On shore a bunch of guys who looked to be in their early twenties were tossing a ball around. One of them missed it, and it flew out over the water. She caught it and tossed it back. At that point they urged her to join them.

Still in pain from Luc's latest cruel strategy to keep his distance from her, she told the guys she would love to. Why not.

They were an odd mixture of Croatians, Germans and Danes, all of whom knew a little English. For the next hour she had a great time while they teased her and laughed over her mispronunciation of words.

The one named Lars told her they were moving on to a discotheque and asked her to come. Though he seemed nice enough, she knew a guy on the make when she saw one.

Claiming fatigue, she declined with a thank you and ran into the water. Not to be daunted, Lars followed after her. By the time she'd reached the *Gabbiano,* he caught hold of one foot as she was climbing the ladder.

"Seriously." She turned to him. "It's late."

"Tomorrow you sleep. Tonight you party."

Before she could say another word, hands of steel gripped her upper arms and lifted her bodily into the boat.

"Take your party elsewhere." Luc's forbidding tone and presence had the guy doing a back flip away from the ladder. He took off like a flying fish.

Olivia had to admit she was relieved. But she refused to give Luc that satisfaction or tell him she was sorry if he'd hurt his leg helping her get away from Mr. Hands. Instead, she hurried below.

Nic was in the galley. She said hi as she rushed past him to get some things out of her suitcase.

After her shower she dried off and put on a new pair of cotton lounging pajamas that were perfectly modest. When she opened the door to the passageway and started for the stairs, Luc was leaning on his cane, blocking her exit.

His eyes played over her damp curls before wandering to her mouth. She could imagine him kissing her like he had done the other night. Her body turned to fire.

"You made a wrong turn. The cabin's the other way."

"I'm going up on deck to enjoy myself."

"Not tonight, and not in that outfit. The deck is Nic's domain after eleven at night. Considering the long day he has put in, he's bushed. Not that you would care about his exhaustion."

It took every bit of willpower to hold on to her control. "Apparently you're not that worried about it, either," she struck back, deriving pleasure from seeing the way his lips formed a pencil-thin line. "I had no way of knowing he would put himself at your disposal at a moment's notice without concern for his own welfare."

"Well now that you do, I suggest you climb up in your bunk so we can all go to sleep."

"You can try," she said in a husky voice. With great daring she raised up on tiptoe to brush her lips against his. "There's more where that came from. All you have to do is call out my name in the night. I promised your mother I would accommodate your every wish."

Frozen gray shards stared back at her. "You didn't fool her you know."

"Of course not. She has to be an exceptional woman to have raised a son as brilliant, troubled, paranoid and dense as you, and still be alive. If Monaco gave out a prize for the best mother in the Principality, she would win hands down. Good night, my proud Falcon who flies alone. Sweet dreams."

She went to bed and pulled the covers over her head. The routine established a pattern for the next three days; sailing lessons interspersed with water sports and good food.

It was the perfect regimen to keep from thinking about Luc who lay around on deck with his nose in a book. Except for spotting her when she went waterskiing, he pretty well ignored her. Any remarks were addressed to Nic. Mostly they discussed theories about who stole the family jewel collection.

In the evenings Nic took Olivia to the local bars and they danced or walked the streets of the little towns of Corniglia, Manarola and Riomaggiore, all part of the Cinque Terre region.

Snorkeling in and around San Remo's grottos had been an especially memorable experience for her. Luc joined them for part of a morning. Though he wasn't any friendlier to her, he seemed to enjoy the exercise and knew all the little secret spots where the tourists didn't go.

The next day they docked at Nice and spent time exploring the Chateau D'Eze positioned thirteen hundred feet above the impossibly blue water. By the time her head touched the pillow that night, she slept the sleep of the exhausted.

Unbeknownst to her, Nic had taken advantage of the wind during the night. While she was oblivious, he'd sailed them past Monaco. When she looked out the window of the cabin the next morning, the unforgettable vista of Cannes lay before her eyes.

She still had a hard time believing she'd been to places on the Riviera she'd only seen in movies and books.

Per usual Luc had gotten up early and prepared their breakfast. Since it involved no heavy lifting, that was the one job he could do using his cane without straining his leg too much.

The three of them ate on deck while the two men

laid out her walking itinerary for the day with Nic. Tomorrow they'd be moving on to Marseilles, then Perpignan. In the days that followed they would sail to the famous ports along the Spanish coast.

Olivia's greatest fear was that they would reach Marbella before Luc showed any sign of wanting to be alone with her. Maybe if she bought him something he would really like, it would soften him up a bit.

When she and Nic went ashore, they spent a full morning sightseeing, but after lunch at the Carlton on the famous La Croisette seafront, she asked him to take her to a book shop that catered to science fiction buffs.

If he thought it a strange request, he didn't say so. For several hours they both poked around the huge store that sold new and used books.

Nic was big into linguistics and heraldry.

During their walks she'd discovered he was an expert on bloodlines and primogeniture. In fact he was writing a book on it in his spare time.

While he found himself some fascinating reading material, she asked the man waiting on her to look up the latest novel about robots. She risked buying Luc something he'd already read, but maybe she'd get lucky.

In the end she bought five books. The most recent one dealt with a robot named Cog. Two other books dealing with artificial intelligence had been published in the last couple of years.

The last two were some of the first books about robots ever published. They dated back to the late eighteen hundreds.

If nothing else, Luc might find them amusing to

read again, if he'd read them, which he probably had. In that case he could have fun picking their research apart.

When Nic joined her at the checkout counter with three books he wanted, she insisted on paying for everything as her way of saying thank you for all his help.

Nic accepted with his usual good grace. At four-thirty they headed back to the *Gabbiano*. Once on board she called down the stairs.

"Yoohoo, Luc. We're back!"

She was excited to see his face when she gave him her gift, but there was no answer. She went below. Maybe he'd fallen asleep.

To her surprise he wasn't in bed. If he'd been swimming around the boat, she would have noticed. A little perplexed, she left the cabin and discovered Nic in the kitchen. He held a piece of paper in his hand.

Beyond his shoulder she noticed Luc's cane lying across the drop table. Olivia's eyes flew to Nic's. Their gazes met.

"He left you a note." The nuance in his tone alarmed her.

Olivia's mouth suddenly went dry. She knew she wasn't going to like what she heard. "W-what does it say?" she stammered.

"I'll let you read it."

CHAPTER NINE

Nic left the kitchen so she could have her privacy.

She put the bag of books on the table. Her hand trembled as she picked up the paper.

My dear Duchess cousin, never let it be said that the Varano cousins didn't honor their obligations to their long lost relations from that upstart nation across the Atlantic.

You're in the best of hands with Nic. He'll make certain the rest of your ten day trip to the French and Spanish portions of the Riviera is fulfilled and memorable.

For Max and Greer's sake, let's agree to go our separate ways without bitterness. I don't want my first day of freedom from prison to be marked by rancor.

Knowing you as I do, you'll probably have success with your new Internet business. After all, you're one of the very unexpected and astounding Duchesses of Kingston.

Luc

She stood there for a long time staring into space. Unexpected and astounding were code words for "freak of nature."

This was the end of the road. She'd gone too far. She'd stepped over an invisible line Luc had drawn long before he'd ever met her. Everyone had tried to warn her, but she hadn't played it like a Duchess.

Scalding tears ran down her cheeks.

"Olivia?" Nic whispered directly behind her.

She wiped at the tears with the back of her hand. "Did you know he was going to leave?"

"Yes. Today the doctor gave him a clean bill of health. Now that he can drive a car again, he's anxious to get on with his life. If you'd known Luc before his accident and realized how much he loved all sports, especially skiing, you would understand how hard it has been for him to be restricted in his physical activities."

"I can imagine." She sniffed. "He's very lucky to have such an understanding cousin who has been his best friend, too. Would you call me a taxi please? I'm going to fly home from Nice today."

"If you'll allow me, I'll ring for a limo and take you to the airport myself."

She loved Nic for not trying to persuade her to continue on with the trip. He would have taken her and shown her the best time in the world. That was because he was kind and honorable.

"What about the *Gabbiano*?"

"I'll arrange for someone to sail it back to Vernazza. All it requires is a phone call."

"Well then. I guess that's it. Excuse me while I pack and get things cleaned up around here." Her glance flicked to the table. "What will you do with his cane?"

"Discard it along with any refuse left on the boat."

"Do you care if I keep it?"

"Of course not."

"Thank you."

Three hours later her overseas flight was announced in the first-class waiting lounge at the Nice airport. The cane had been taken away as a security precaution and would be given to her once she landed at Kennedy airport in New York.

Nic gave her one last hug. "Have a safe flight. Give my regards to your sister."

"I will." She raised tear-filled eyes to his. "The next time you see Luc, will you make sure he gets these books? Tell him—" She bit her lip. "Tell him they're a peace offering from me."

He gave her a solemn nod before striding out of the lounge.

"Etienne? Have you seen my brother?"

The dark-blond chief mechanic who'd hit on Olivia looked up from the under-chassis he was working on.

"Luc!" He got to his feet and started wiping his greasy hands with a rag. "No one has seen you around here in a long time. Look at you—walking as if you were never in that accident. Congratulations."

"*Merci,* Etienne."

"It must feel good."

"It does, believe me. Is my brother around?"

"He's out testing the new wheels we put on his car."

"How long do you think he will be?"

"Another hour maybe, but if you need to talk to him, I'll tell him to come in."

"I'd appreciate that."

"Of course. *Un moment,*" he said before disappearing.

Luc had called the villa in Positano when he hadn't been able to reach Cesar on his cell phone. Bianca told him he'd gone back to Monaco to start training for his next race.

That explained why Luc hadn't been able to make contact. It was one of their mother's greatest concerns that when Cesar was at the track, he didn't check his voice mail until the end of the day. For once Luc could understand her frustration since it was imperative he talk to his brother. The conversation that should have taken place two years ago couldn't be put off a moment longer.

Before Luc had hung up with Bianca, he'd chatted with her for a few minutes, asking her how things were going. Never one to hold back with an opinion, she launched into a backlog of news about her family and friends, the dog next door that was such a nuisance.

And speaking of nuisances, she'd had to throw out one of Cesar's fans who was insane enough to come to the villa. When Luc commented that he thought Cesar brought women there after every race, she started raging at him for suggesting such a thing.

Luc asked her why she was so upset. She pretended not to understand and said she needed to get off the phone, but he wouldn't let her go. When he accused her of keeping a secret from him, she cried out he would have to ask Cesar.

"If you're talking about Genevieve, I already know about it, Bianca."

The older housekeeper had sounded shocked. Then she'd broken down in tears before it all came gushing out, verifying everything Olivia had alluded to.

As Luc listened, his throat swelled in pain for his silent accusations against his brother, for the two years Bianca had kept her silence.

Because Luc had believed Genevieve's lies, he'd refused to let Cesar explain. In consequence their family had suffered needlessly. With hindsight Luc could see that his intransigence had spilled over to his cousins who'd been forced to tread softly around him.

"Luc?"

At the sound of his brother's voice, he turned in his direction.

"Your cane—it's gone! You must be three inches taller!" The joy in Cesar's voice was so heartfelt, Luc felt crucified all over again for the injury he'd caused his brother.

Cesar stood in the doorway, still wearing his driver's suit. His dark hair was mussed from the helmet he'd been wearing. It took Luc back years to a time when they were young boys playing Space soldiers.

Pere Noel had brought them spacemen costumes for Christmas. Luc had immediately transformed his into a robot suit. No matter how many times Cesar begged to wear it, Luc wouldn't let him.

Olivia had accused him of always having to be in charge, like Greer. At the time he'd laughed off her comment, but he wasn't laughing now. Without Luc realizing it, Cesar had grown up to be one of the world's great Formula I drivers and a successful businessman in his own right.

But he was a lot more than that. Luc realized he was looking at the greatest brother a man could ever have. If it hadn't been for Olivia...

"How about taking a ride with *me* for a change, *mon frère?*"

There was a palpable silence while Cesar's gaze

searched his. He must have seen the pleading in Luc's because he suddenly broke into a grin.

"I don't know. It's been a while since you've sat behind the wheel of a car, but I'm willing to risk it considering it's you." The last came out in a husky tone.

Luc studied his brother. He didn't deserve this second chance, but because Cesar was the better man, Luc was getting it. "If I've forgotten how, I know I've got the best there is to help me."

"Etienne? I'm taking off with my brother!" Cesar shouted with the kind of excitement Luc hadn't heard in years. "Don't plan on seeing me until you see me!"

"…so what do you think? Try to picture them polished smooth."

Piper stared at the rocks laid out on the counter in the kitchen. Then her glance shifted to Olivia. "They're pretty."

"No, they're not. You're just saying that to make me feel better."

Her sister cocked her head. "In theory I think your idea to sell them for paperweights is terrific. Tell you what. Let's get in the car and go to that lapidary shop on Decater Avenue. We'll ask whoever's in charge to give us their honest opinion."

Olivia lowered her head. "They won't be honest. They're out to make money and will probably tell me the end product will look like jewels."

Piper poured them both a glass of milk to drink with their sandwiches. She brought them to the table. "You know what I think?"

"What?" Olivia asked before biting into her bologna and cheese.

"You're beginning to sound as cynical as someone else I could mention."

"I don't want to talk about him."

"Then how come you brought home his cane?"

The last bite Olivia took tasted like sawdust. "It'll serve as a reminder of my terrible judgment. Did I tell you I'm never going to Europe again?"

"In a year's time you won't feel so awful."

"What's happening in a year?"

"Greer and Max's first wedding anniversary. I'm sure they'll throw a big party and we'll be expected to come."

"I have a better idea. We'll have one for them here. A picnic. Just the four of us. Waterskiing on the Hudson."

"In whose boat? We can't ask Fred or Tom."

"We'll rent one."

Piper finished off the second half of her sandwich. "Maybe between both our businesses, we can make enough money this year to buy our own boat."

"Yeah." Olivia would love to prove to Luc she'd made her fortune.

"Come on. Let's go see a man about a rock polisher."

Olivia drained the last of her milk, then got up from the table. "Thanks for coming with me."

"It's all for one, remember?"

When she felt her sister give her a hug, Olivia lost it. "I disgust him, Piper."

"No, you don't. It's the situation that shut him down emotionally. His fiancée committed the unpardonable betrayal by approaching his brother. When you came along and showed so much interest in Cesar, Luc thought he was being betrayed again and you received the brunt of his pain.''

''But Luc was the one who introduced us! He didn't have to.''

''Of course he did. Sooner or later you would have found out Cesar Villon was Luc's brother. When you were already angry with Luc and his cousins for what they did to us, how would you have felt about Luc once you found out he'd kept *that* information from you?''

Olivia looked at her sister through eyes drowning in tears. Since the answer was obvious, there was no point in responding.

''Luc was trying to make up to you for the bad time he and his cousins put us through. It was simply a ghastly coincidence that he found out your greatest wish in coming to Europe was to watch Cesar race in the Grand Prix.''

''But not all women racing fans are groupies,'' she exclaimed before burying her face in her hands.

''Of course not. You just happened to fall in love with the wrong man. Max was worried for you, so he told Greer about Luc. When Nic could see you were starting to care too much, he confided similar fears to me. Unfortunately their warnings came too late.''

''How humiliating.'' Olivia's whole body shuddered.

''Don't dwell on it anymore.''

''That's easy for you to say. Mother and Daddy were right about me. I always have to learn everything the hard way.''

''I learned a painful lesson myself this last trip.''

Olivia's head lifted. ''What do you mean?''

"When I saw you drive off with Cesar after the wedding, I thought I'd try to get a proposal out of Nic. You know, so I could laugh and tell him sorry, wrong duchess. He's such a know-it-all, I wanted to give him a hard time."

"And?"

"It was a big mistake."

They left the apartment and hurried out to their dad's old Pontiac. Olivia got in the driver's seat and started the car. Once they'd joined the mainstream of traffic she asked, "How big?"

"I guess you could say I made the worst faux pas of my life by getting him to try to come on to me a little bit. We'd been walking on the grounds. I asked him to show me where he used to play when he and Luc visited Max.

"He took me to a stream with an old waterwheel that had stopped working long ago. You remember how hot it was that day. I suggested we take a little nap together under the trees. No one was around."

Olivia would have been scandalized if she hadn't tried to do virtually the same thing to Luc on the *Gabbiano*. "Go on."

"Well, I lifted my arms to help him take off his tux jacket. But he grabbed my hands and pushed me away."

"He didn't physically hurt you did he?" Olivia couldn't believe they were talking about the same Nic.

Piper bit her lip. "No. He did something a lot worse. He explained he was wearing a black armband for a reason. But because I was one of the notorious Duchesses of Kingston, he would excuse me this once for not knowing how to behave in polite society."

"You've got to be kidding me."

"No. I thought it was a joke, too, until he made it clear that his family and the family of his deceased fiancée Nina were in official mourning until next April. If you recall, his dad was wearing an armband at the wedding, and at the party in Monaco."

By now Olivia was so hurt for her sister, she was ready to throw rocks. "How dare he speak to you like that after the way he flirted with you on the *Piccione!* He wasn't wearing an armband then!"

"Ah—that was different. The Varano cousins were working undercover to expose us as jewel thieves."

"So it's okay to take it off while in the line of duty. What a hypocrite!"

"I smiled and told him he'd just passed up an experience he would live to regret. Then I walked back to the villa and had a limo take me to the train. After buying a one-way ticket, I headed for Genoa. What an irony when you consider Tom would have given anything if I'd thrown myself at him like that."

By now Olivia's tears had dried up. "I'm sorry I wasn't there for you. I was too busy trying to make Luc jealous to think about anyone but myself."

"We were both idiots. It was probably a reaction to losing Greer."

"I'm sure you're right."

Olivia spied the Arrowhead Rock Shop on the corner and pulled into the parking area around the back. Within twenty minutes she returned to the car carrying a tumbler that vibrated. Piper followed with some packages of polish and three barrels to hold the rocks for each stage of the process.

Once back at the apartment, Olivia set up her paraphernalia in the kitchen and got started. Every so often Piper came in from the living room to see how things were going.

"I won't know what I've got here until we go to bed."

At eleven she checked her first batch. The rocks had disappeared. They'd been pulverized.

When she thought things couldn't get any worse, the phone rang.

Piper checked the caller ID. Her mouth tightened. "It's out of area."

"It could be Greer."

"No. We already spoke to her earlier today. This late I bet it's Nic. He put you on the plane yesterday. He knows what Luc did to you was unconscionable. No doubt he wants to know if you got home safely."

Olivia rolled her eyes. "That'll be his excuse, but what he really wants is to hear *your* voice."

"He's in mourning, remember?" Piper snapped.

Angry for her sister's sake, Olivia reached for the receiver. "I'll take this call with the greatest of pleasure."

After waiting five rings, she picked up. Using a heavy Bronx accent she said, "You want the Duchesses of Kingston? Leave yohur name and phone numbah. If yoh're lucky you might hear back from us, but it'll prwabably be next yeahr."

As soon as she hung up the receiver they both laughed hysterically. They were still giggling out of control when they climbed into their own beds. Then the tears started, drenching Olivia's pillow.

"She's home."

His expression grim, Luc folded his cell phone and put it back in his pocket.

On the heels of his relief that Olivia had arrived safely in New York loomed the growing fear that he'd done too much damage and she'd never be able to forgive him. Knowing she wasn't aboard the *Gabbiano* filled him with a gnawing emptiness.

A steady breeze had kept the sail filled during the night. Now he and Nic were in the waters of the Costa del Sol. The sun had been up several hours. Marbella lay off the starboard bow.

The plan he'd discussed with Nic during the night had to work, or his life really wouldn't have any meaning.

When they reached Nic's private dock, some workmen he'd alerted on the estate ahead of time were on hand to greet them.

Nic made the introductions. "Thank you for coming so quickly."

"You said you were in a hurry, Senor de Pastrana. What is it you wish to have done?"

"Luc has just purchased this boat and wants it painted flame-blue and white so it looks brand-new. Another sail has been ordered and will be delivered day after tomorrow to match the new name he'd like painted on it.

"He's in charge. While he gives you details, I'm going up to the villa to attend to some business and will talk to you later."

The men nodded.

Within a half hour Luc had instructed them on everything he wanted done. They promised to get a full crew assembled to finish the job as quickly as possible.

Since time was of the essence, Luc couldn't have

asked for more than that. When he joined Nic in his study, his cousin was seated at the computer.

"Any luck tracking down Signore Tozetti?"

"His secretary said he just came in his office and would join us at any moment. I've set it up for a conference call. Go ahead and use my cell phone."

Luc sat down on one of the love seats and put the phone to his ear while he waited. Another minute passed, then they heard a voice.

"Signore Tozetti here. Good morning, gentlemen."

"Good morning."

"It's a great honor to be speaking to members of the House of Parma-Bourbon. What can I do for you?"

"The owners of Duchesse Designs, the American women whose calendars you are planning to distribute throughout the Parma region, happen to be distant cousins of ours."

"I had no idea. They never intimated—"

"That doesn't surprise us, *signore*. They believe in themselves and their product. My cousin and I believe in their product, too, and that's the reason we're calling. We want to back them. Therefore we have a proposition to make to you."

"Wonderful! What exactly did you have in mind?"

"We'd like to see their calendars distributed in other countries besides Italy. If you are interested in being in charge of the total distribution, it would work to everyone's advantage."

A laugh of surprised delight sounded over the wires. "I would be very interested, *signore*. What countries besides Italy are you thinking of?"

"Monaco, France, Spain to begin with."

"Have their calendars already been printed in French and Spanish?"

"These are points we need to talk about. Could you meet with us for a late lunch today at the restaurant of the Splendido in Portofino, say two o'clock?"

"Of course."

"We'll talk serious business then. It's vital you present the offer you're going to make to them in such a way, they feel it's a hundred percent genuine."

"I'll do my best."

"You'll have to," Luc said emotionally. "Money doesn't drive them, so promising them the moon will be a turnoff. Naturally they're in the business to make a living, but the pigeon drawings of Violetta and Luigio happen to be very near and dear to their hearts.

"When you make your pitch, you'll have to convince them the words and depictions representing those lovebirds speak to your soul."

"I don't understand. You make it sound like they might turn me down!"

"That's because they're *artistes*. No matter how much they want to be a success, they have to know you believe in their work. If you can do that, then they'll agree to meet you for the signing of the contract wherever you say."

"You mean they won't be coming to Genoa?"

"No. We'll tell you more this afternoon. But there is one stipulation we must make before things go any further."

"What is that?"

"Our cousins must never know we approached you. Our names must never be mentioned or come up in future conversations. The entire project will fail and you will lose the business you already have with them if they even get a hint anyone else is involved. *Capisce?*"

After a long silence, *"Capisce."*

Piper turned to a fresh page on her drawing pad and began sketching. "How much time before we have to meet with Signore Tozetti at the hotel?"

Olivia had been looking up at the incredible wood-carved ceiling of the world famous Alhambra. Now they'd come out to the reflecting pool in the garden. "We've got about a half hour until dinner. It's already seven."

"Three days in Spain haven't given me very long to work up a decent presentation. My hand has a cramp."

"He said he didn't expect a finished product. All he wants are samples he can show the man who's willing to print our calendars here in Spain. If they prove to be as outstanding as the drawings you did of Monaco and Parma, then we'll have another outlet."

. "I wish I could flesh them out more, but there isn't time."

Moving closer, Olivia looked over Piper's shoulder. "In my opinion, this grouping is the best you've ever done."

"You say that every time I start a new sketch"

"That's because you're a genius."

"No. It's because I'm seeing everything live rather than having to depend on photographs."

"Even so, Luigio and Violetta have always been products of your imagination and you've captured a new look for both of them."

"I have?"

"Yes. The one of him as a toreador, trailing his cape around Seville's corrida in front of Violetta is priceless. He has a proud, autocratic bearing about him that makes my heart race."

"You think?"

"Absolutely. Violetta's different, too. She has a crueler smile while they're dancing the flamenco in those fabulous outfits. And I love the seductive angle of his hat.

"Honestly Piper, you've caught the atmosphere of that cave we visited last night so perfectly, I can almost hear their heels clicking on the wooden floor. There's a sensual appeal that leaps out from the page."

"Thanks."

"I mean it. I also love that other drawing of him standing on the turreted rampart of the Alcazar in Segovia, staring up at Violetta who's leaning out one of the windows. They're the most romantic-looking pair I've ever seen. You can feel that tragic quality about him that melts my heart. As if he'd been pierced to the quick by love, but she's still holding out."

Piper kept her face averted. Though Luigio was the male pigeon, Olivia knew her sister identified with his feelings.

So did Olivia...

"Mother and Daddy would be so proud to know your drawings are going to be famous all over Europe."

"We don't know that yet," Piper muttered, "so let's not count our chickens."

"Signore Tozetti wouldn't have paid us an advance to come here if he didn't believe he was going to make a bundle off you pretty soon. When he sees what you've done in just three days, he'll be sending you everywhere…France—Switzerland—''

Piper lifted her head. ''What do you mean *me?* This was Greer's brainchild, and if you hadn't done all the East Coast marketing in the first place, we wouldn't have a calendar business period. We're in this together!

''Let's just be thankful Greer had the foresight to suggest we try to market our idea when we first arrived in Genoa. You and I may not have succeeded in getting a proposal out of a Riviera playboy, but we could end up making a very nice living for ourselves by the time we're thirty.''

''That would be an irony, wouldn't it?'' Olivia laughed sadly. ''Greer was the one who didn't want us to marry for fear it would get in the way of our making money.''

''Yup. Now's she's got a fantastic husband and doesn't have to earn her own living.''

''Yup. And my paperweight idea went down the tubes to the tune of one hundred eighty dollars.''

''Hey—you didn't know those rocks were volcanic ash.''

''Luc did.''

''Forget him. If we make it to France, we'll go to that quarry Victor Hugo wrote about in *Les Miserables.* You know, the place where Jean Valjean was a prisoner. We'll take a bunch of rocks home from there and polish them into beads. You can sell those over the Internet. All isn't lost yet!''

''You're being very sweet, Piper, but I'm pretty sure that place doesn't exist, either. I think we'd better head for the hotel.''

Piper drew a long-stemmed rose peeking out from

Luigio's wing. He was hiding it from Violetta, and would give it to her later. Olivia thought it the perfect touch. Then her sister closed her sketchpad and stood up. "Let's go."

The hotel was only a five-minute walk from the entrance. "Don't be nervous," Olivia reminded her.

"I'm not nervous."

"Yes, you are. You're practically mowing all the tourists down."

Before long they entered the luxury hotel and looked around the Moorish-styled foyer for Signore Tozetti.

"I don't see him."

"Neither do I."

"Maybe he's in the bar."

"In that case he would have told someone at the front desk. Let's find out."

"Oh, yes," the man said. "We've been calling your names. Signore Tozetti has met with a minor accident and won't be able to join you until tomorrow morning at our sister hotel in Malaga."

Her eyes swerved to Piper's. Malaga wasn't that far from the Pastrana villa in Marbella, a fact both of them were agonizingly aware of. The very mention of it brought back bittersweet memories of Olivia's disastrous trips with Luc.

There'd been so many stops and starts without ever once making it all the way to the Spanish Riviera. In her dreams he was supposed to have ended up proposing to her. The pain was almost more than she could bear.

"He's very sorry for the inconvenience and has arranged to have you driven there this evening by limousine. He hopes that will meet with your approval. Shall I send someone for your bags?''

The silence lengthened. Piper, who was as disappointed as Olivia that their meeting had been postponed, finally had the presence of mind to say yes.

Within ten minutes they walked through the arcaded entry to the portico. A uniformed chauffeur helped them into the most luxurious black limousine Olivia had ever seen. Smoked glass windows. All shiny mahogany and leather on the inside.

The closed partition between the occupants and driver guaranteed total privacy. You could lie down on the seats and still have wiggle room for your feet.

''Have you ever seen such an elegant limousine?'' Piper commented after it pulled into traffic.

''No. It must be a Spanish design.''

''The world's best kept secret. We could use limos like this in New York. I wonder why we haven't seen any?''

Olivia leaned her head back against the plush seat. ''I'll give you one guess.''

''You're right. This thing probably costs close to a half a million dollars.''

''Probably more.''

''Signore Tozetti has gone all out for us. He must really want our business. Kind of makes you wonder why.''

Olivia felt the hairs stand on the back of her neck. ''I agree. Don't get me wrong. Your artwork is fabulous, but—''

''But not that fabulous,'' Piper finished the sentence for her.

''Do you remember when we first boarded the *Piccione?*''

"You're reading my mind. Greer sensed something was wrong, but we didn't believe her. Not at first."

"By the time she'd convinced us we were in trouble, it was too late to get off."

"Don't look now, but there aren't any door handles or window buttons."

Olivia felt madly for them, but nothing was there. She jerked around and tried to slide the partition so she could see to talk to the driver. It wouldn't budge.

She pounded on it with the flat of her hand.

By now Piper had joined her on the seat. "Stop the car! We want to get out!" she shouted.

Suddenly an interior light went on while the limo was still moving. Classical music began to play softly in the background. A panel lifted on one side of the car to reveal a magnum of champagne on ice and two glasses.

"Good evening, earthwomen. My name is Cog."

CHAPTER TEN

COG?

Olivia's world reeled on its axis.

"Oh my gosh—there really are UFOs!" Piper cried out in absolute panic. "We're being abducted and taken to an alien spaceship."

"Hardly," Olivia mocked after she'd had a few seconds to recover. But her heart was beating so fast with excitement, her body was literally shaking. "Did you ever hear of an alien who spoke with a French accent? A mad scientist maybe, but not an alien.

"And this particular madman just got his driving privileges back so he has gone berserk!"

As recognition dawned, Piper's expression underwent a fundamental change. "You say his name is Cog?" she played along. "What does it stand for? Creature of Godzilla?"

"Close. Literally Cog means he's the subordinate brainchild of his deranged creator, trained to do necessary but minor tasks."

"You mean like pour us a glass of that champagne?"

"All you had to do was ask," Cog spoke again.

Like magic a cork remover appeared and they heard a pop. When it disappeared, a clamp shot out around the neck of the bottle, lifted it and poured champagne into both glasses without spilling a drop. Then it put the bottle back in the bucket and disappeared.

Delighted, Olivia reached for the glasses and handed one to Piper.

"Cog? My sister's starving because Signore Tozetti didn't show up for dinner. By the way, just how much did your mad creator pay him to lure us across the ocean?"

"I know nothing about my master's private business. What does your sister require?"

"What have you got?"

A panel on the other side of the car went up to expose a plate with half a dozen roll-ups in individual napkins. "What are they?"

"Spanish tortillas."

Piper handed her one because she was closest. It was hot. Olivia bit into it. Um. "Not bad, Cog."

After her sister took one and started munching, the panel closed.

"So where are you taking us?"

"To the mother ship."

"Why?"

"To talk of new possibilities."

At this point her heart had jumped to her throat. "It's too late for that. Your master destroyed the world I live in."

"There are other worlds."

"I'm talking about the human world. The only one I want. You know. Emotions. Hearts. Souls. Flesh. Blood. Guts. Tears. All that good stuff."

"My master made a mistake in judgment."

"I thought the masters of your universe couldn't calculate incorrectly. It just goes to show you everything I ever believed in is a myth."

"He wants another chance to restore your faith."

"Faith? Such a word isn't part of that madman's vocabulary. He's just a robot like you."

"Cog does not know what robot means. Please explain."

"Take a good look at your master and you'll have your answer."

"I only obey him. He has ordered me to bring you to him."

"That's too bad. I'm not going."

"I *must* produce you."

"What happens if you don't?"

"He will self destruct, and that will be the end of Cog."

"Don't worry about it. You're no great shakes. I know a robot that can drive two thousand miles through enemy lines delivering medicine."

"He said you would be difficult."

"Yeah, well he doesn't know the half of it!"

"Give in," Piper whispered. "Can't you see he's dying?"

Piper was such a romantic. That was because of her artistic genes. "You're just like mother."

"That's not such a bad thing you know," Piper muttered in a hurt voice. "She had Daddy eating out of her hand."

"I'd rather be eating out of Cog's hand. What do you have for dessert? I might be willing to negotiate a few terms if you've got something chocolate."

Another panel on Olivia's side flew up to reveal a plate of them. She reached for a dark chocolate truffle and bit into it.

"Hmm. That's yummy. Here, Piper. This one's milk chocolate."

"Do you wish anything else?"

"Not for now, Cog."

The panel closed.

She could feel them traveling down a slope and around several curves. Then the limo came to a full stop.

"We have arrived at the ship."

Olivia's heart was ready to burst from its cavity.

"Please step out of the car."

The door flew open on her side to reveal a glorious stretch of beach. Trembling because she knew Luc was waiting for her, she got to her feet and climbed out, expecting him to pull her into his arms. She would put up an initial struggle, then cave.

But to her surprise he was nowhere around. All she could see was a private pier and a sailboat.

Good grief. Had the car actually driven them here by itself? Her legs started to buckle.

"Piper?" she murmured.

There was no answer.

"Piper?" She cried and wheeled around.

No one. Nothing. It was as if her sister had disappeared off the face of the earth. All she could see was dense foliage interspersed with gorgeous flowering trees of all kinds.

"Luc?" She was starting to get nervous. "Luc?" she cried louder.

"I'm over here."

Cog's voice had been replaced by the real thing.

Her eyes swerved back to the pier. There he stood. Tall and rock solid. You would never know he'd had to rely on a cane for so many months.

"Come aboard the *Olivier*."

That was the name he called her in French. His compelling male voice had her walking to the pier.

She stopped a few feet short of him. In well-worn denims and a white crew neck cotton sweater, his powerful male body was so appealing, she averted her hungry eyes.

"I—it kind of looks like the *Gabbiano,*" she faltered.

"It *is* the *Gabbiano.* But when you sailed her, you made her your own, so I bought it from Giovanni to give to you."

Her breath caught in her throat. "I would have thought this was a brand-new sailboat. I love the blue color."

"It matches your eyes."

Luc—

"Someone did a beautiful job restoring it."

"Thank you."

"You?" she cried.

He gave an elegant shrug of his broad shoulders. "I had help. It's my peace offering to you. The first step in delicate negotiations."

"For what purpose?"

"To see if we can't find a new starting point."

Pain knifed through her once more. "That would be impossible. I'm your brother's pit babe, remember? Because if you don't, I can give you chapter and verse of every cruel thing you ever said to me."

"Don't, Olivia," he begged. Incredibly when she looked in his eyes, she saw pain and pleading.

"Don't what?" her voice shook. "Have you any idea what it's like to be compared to a piece of fruit everyone has picked over? A fruit rotten at its core?"

She could see his throat working. "You *know* I never meant any of those things, *mon amour.* You've got to hear me out.'' The pleading in his voice was a revelation to Olivia. "I had a long talk with Cesar.''

"For his sake I'm thankful—'' she blurted, unable to hold back after so much suffering. "He deserved to be let out of the prison you put him in when you wouldn't let him explain anything. If anyone understands what that feels like, I do.''

"There are different kinds of prisons. I'd like the chance to tell you about mine while we take the *Olivier* out for a sail. This will be her maiden voyage under her new name and colors.''

Oh, Luc.

He could make her do anything. Greer would tell her she had no spine. But like the pushover she was, she let him help her into the boat. Before jumping in after her with an agility he hadn't been able to demonstrate before now, he untied the ropes.

She put on the life jacket he handed her. Soon he revved the motor and they made their way to open water.

"Would you like to do the honors?'' he asked after cutting the engine.

She walked over to the mast and released the sail. The night breeze filled it.

"Oh—'' she cried softly when she saw the stylized design, against the white, of a graceful olive tree whose branches reached out in every direction.

Luc—

He came to stand by her. They guided the sail together. "While I was at that robotics seminar at M.I.T., I noticed a message from Genevieve on my voice mail that said she'd been at the hospital and wanted me to come home quick.

"I couldn't imagine what had happened, and she'd

turned off her phone. I flew back to Nice and drove straight to her apartment only to learn that she'd had a miscarriage.''

Olivia moaned.

"It came as a tremendous shock because I'd taken precautions and didn't have a clue she was pregnant. She admitted it wasn't mine. Then she confessed to having had a secret affair with Cesar before getting engaged to me.

"She knew it was his baby and had gone to see him since he needed to be told the truth before she broke her engagement to me. According to her story, Cesar wanted nothing to do with her and said it was her problem. His rejection brought on her miscarriage.''

"And you believed her over the brother you'd known all your life?" Olivia cried.

"No. Not until the hospital did a follow-up call while I was there to make certain she had someone taking care of her. Apparently she lost a lot of blood. When I asked the attending physician the age of the fetus, he told me ten weeks.

"I'd only started having relations with her after our engagement a month earlier. That meant it couldn't be mine. I walked away from her and never looked back. But I still couldn't believe it was Cesar's child. If he'd been interested in her, I would have known about it before she came to my office looking for a job.

"Because I was so certain she'd lied about my brother's involvement with her, I sent a friend to the garage to learn what he could. Mechanics love to gossip. All it took was a few glasses of wine for Etienne to admit Cesar and Genevieve had been a hot item for a while. The date for the baby's conception fit.''

Now it was Olivia who was feeling sick.

Luc's eyes grew bleak. ''That began a nightmare from which I never awakened until you forced me to rethink the situation. Olivia,'' he whispered. His hands slid up her arms. She could hear his shallow breathing, feel it together with the wind on her lips.

''If you hadn't provoked me, I would never have gone to my brother to learn the truth. I heard some of it from Bianca, then he repeated to me exactly what he told you, and a lot more.''

''A lot more?'' she asked emotionally.

''Yes.'' His hands tightened on shoulders. ''I found out he toyed with you about an engagement ring to test your love for me.''

''Yes, darling.'' Her eyes filled. ''He loves you that much. He's an amazing brother.''

''He is.'' Olivia heard him clear his throat. ''After we'd made our peace, we confronted Etienne.''

''The mechanic you thought I was after,'' she said in a wounded voice.

''I didn't really believe it, Olivia. I swear to you I didn't, but I was in so much pain over you I became the madman you accused me of being.''

She wiped her eyes. ''Did Etienne admit he'd lied about Cesar's affair with your fiancée?''

Luc's body hardened. ''He admitted far more. Genevieve was a fortune-hunting groupie. Unbeknownst to Cesar or me, she gave Etienne her favors to get information on the Falcon family before she entered our lives.

''Genevieve's plan was to go after me because she thought I had more money. But her plans backfired because she discovered she was pregnant with Etienne's baby.''

''What?''

''It gets ugly. When she told Etienne she was carrying his child and was afraid I would find out because the dates were wrong, he told her to get rid of it. She refused and decided to play up to Cesar, hoping that if they slept together one time, she could pin it on him and he would marry her in the end.''

''That's ghastly! Now I'm beginning to understand your venom. How could a woman do that?''

His eyes glittered silver. ''It happens. But as you know, Cesar sent her packing and told her that if she didn't tell me she'd approached him, he would tell me himself.

''When nothing worked out as she'd planned, she turned on Etienne and blackmailed him into giving her money to get rid of the baby, or she'd tell his wife. There were complications from the procedure and she ended up at the hospital.''

''It's a horror story.'' Her hands slid up to his face. ''I hope they both suffer agony for what they did to you and Cesar.''

He covered her hands with his own. ''Etienne no longer has a job with Cesar of course. But my brother's the best man I know. He doesn't want Etienne's family to suffer, so he gave him a good recommendation for finding another mechanic's job.''

''I love Cesar for that.''

''So do I. As for Genevieve, what goes around, comes around. The point is, my brother and I are closer than ever. It's all because of you.''

He shook his dark, handsome head. ''I loved you from the beginning, and that love grew while you fought for our love. You do love me.'' He shook her gently. ''I know you do, *mon coeur.*''

''So much it's killing me. Oh, Luc—when I returned to the boat with Nic and found you'd gone for good, I thought I was going to die.''

His lips roamed over her face. ''I had to leave and take care of my past. How else could I offer you a future.''

''I know that now.''

Unable to suppress her needs any longer, she gave him her mouth. They clung fiercely, forgetting everything in the joy of being together without strife as a constant companion.

She drowned in rapture as his mouth began devouring hers. Neither of them could get close enough. After that terrible day in Cannes when she thought her world had come to an end, she never dreamed Luc had gone off in search of the truth.

Olivia was still having a hard time believing the war was over, that she was claiming the spoils of victory and Luc was helping her with a possessive eagerness.

''Whoa—'' she cried and laughed at the same time as the boat started to list to the other side sending salt spray over them.

Luc grasped her tighter while he grabbed hold of the sail. ''It's time to take the boat back to shore.''

''But we just came out here!''

''There's something else we have to do first. Then we'll take off and let the wind blow us wherever it will.''

''I'd love that, but what could be more important than being together right now?''

"Getting married first," he whispered against her lips before giving her a deep, salty kiss.

When he finally let her go she blurted, "You mean now? Tonight?" Her voice came out with a definite squeak.

He smiled the smile she lived for, making her heart race. "Am I to presume that was a happy 'yes' coming out of the unexpected and astounding Duchess of Kingston?"

Though he'd said it teasingly, she detected the tiniest trace of anxiety in the question. Her darling Luc was having equal trouble believing their pain was behind them.

"Yes!" She threw her arms around his neck and gave him another long, passionate kiss. "Yes, yes, yes. I want to marry you this instant, but we need a church and a priest. Mother and Daddy were very insistent on that."

"I happen to be insistent on it myself." A mysterious gleam had entered his eyes. "All we have to do is get in the limo and drive to the Pastrana family chapel where Father Torres is waiting. Then I'm taking you away with me."

"How long a drive is it?"

"About one minute."

"One minute? That doesn't give me time to make myself presentable. Darling—I really like your mother and I know it will hurt her horribly if she and your father don't get to see you married."

"They'll live."

She bit her lip. "There's another problem."

"What's that?" He kissed the end of her proud Duchess nose.

"Cesar might feel left out to miss his only brother's nuptials."

"He'll live, too."

"Luc—I—I'm afraid Greer and Piper will never forgive me if I exclude them."

His eyes flashed silver fire. "So that's what your hesitation is all about. Max was right. You three really are joined at the mind, heart and hip."

"Only for the important occasions. Weddings, births an—"

His mouth crushed hers before she could say anything else. "Do you love me?" he finally asked.

"You know I do!"

"Then trust me."

Trust.

There was something in the way he said it that told her he was going to make her every wish come true. Lucien de Falcon was that kind of man.

"I'll trust if you'll tell me one thing honestly."

"Anything for my bride-to-be."

"Were you at the wheel during the drive from Granada?"

He threw his dark head back and laughed. It was the most beautiful sound in the world.

"Was that a 'yes'?"

"When I'm your husband, then I'll tell you everything you want to know." With her clasped in his arms, he brought the boat around and they headed for shore, breathlessly awaiting their future.

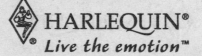

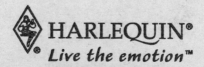

Harlequin Romance®

*Every month, sample the fresh new talent in
Harlequin Romance®!
For sparkling, emotional, feel-good romance, try:*

January 2005
Marriage Make-Over, #3830
by *Ally Blake*

February 2005
Hired by Mr. Right, #3834
by *Nicola Marsh*

March 2005
For Our Children's Sake, #3838
by *Natasha Oakley*

April 2005
The Bridal Bet, #3842
by *Trish Wylie*

The shining new stars of tomorrow!

Available wherever Harlequin books are sold.

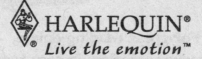

HARLEQUIN®
Live the emotion™

www.eHarlequin.com

HRNTA1204